"How in the world did you convince me to marry you?" Eloise asked him.

"I didn't. You proposed to me," Jonah replied.

A flush of embarrassment traveled up her neck. "I proposed to you?"

He squared his shoulders with defiant pride. "Yes."

"If you try to tell me I got down on my knees and begged, I'll call you a liar."

The hint of a grin played at one corner of his mouth. "It was more like a business proposal. You said you wanted a husband."

"I just barged into your home one day and said I wanted a husband?" she choked out, her embarrassment multiplying.

"It kind of surprised me, too," he admitted.

Dear Reader,

Welcome to the fourth great month of CELEBRATION 1000! We're winding up this special event with fireworks!— six more dazzling love stories that will light up your summer nights. The festivities begin with *Impromptu Bride* by beloved author Annette Broadrick. While running for their lives, Graham Douglas and Katie Kincaid had to marry. But will their hasty wedding lead to everlasting love?

Favorite author Elizabeth August will keep you enthralled with *The Forgotten Husband.* Amnesia keeps Eloise from knowing the real reason she'd married rugged, brooding Jonah Tavish. But brief memories of sweet passion keep her searching for the truth.

This month our FABULOUS FATHER is *Daniel's Daddy*— a heartwarming story by Stella Bagwell.

Debut author Kate Thomas brings us a tale of courtship— Texas-style in—*The Texas Touch.*

There's love and laughter when a runaway heiress plays *Stand-in Mom* in Susan Meier's romantic romp. And don't miss Jodi O'Donnell's emotional story of a love all but forgotten in *A Man To Remember.*

We'd love to know if you have enjoyed CELEBRATION 1000! Please write to us at the address shown below.

Happy reading!

Anne Canadeo
Senior Editor

Please address questions and book requests to:
Silhouette Reader Service
U.S.: 3010 Walden Ave., P.O. Box 1325, Buffalo, NY 14269
Canadian: P.O. Box 609, Fort Erie, Ont. L2A 5X3

Elizabeth August
THE FORGOTTEN HUSBAND

Silhouette
ROMANCE™
Published by Silhouette Books
America's Publisher of Contemporary Romance

To Tara Gavin and Anne Canadeo,
for their support and encouragement

SILHOUETTE BOOKS

ISBN 0-373-19019-0

THE FORGOTTEN HUSBAND

This edition published by arrangement with Harlequin Enterprises B.V.

® and TM are trademarks of Harlequin Enterprises B.V., used under license. Trademarks indicated with ® are registered in the United States Patent and Trademark Office, the Canadian Trade Marks Office and in other countries.

Printed in U.S.A.

Books by Elizabeth August

Silhouette Romance

Author's Choice #554
Truck Driving Woman #590
Wild Horse Canyon #626
Something So Right #668
The Nesting Instinct #719
Joey's Father #749
Ready-Made Family #771
The Man from Natchez #790
A Small Favor #809
The Cowboy and the Chauffeur #833
Like Father, Like Son #857
The Wife He Wanted #881
The Virgin Wife #921
Haunted Husband #922
Lucky Penny #945
A Wedding for Emily #953
The Seeker #989
†*The Forgotten Husband* #1019

Silhouette Special Edition

One Last Fling! #871

*Smytheshire, Massachusetts Series
†Where The Heart Is

ELIZABETH AUGUST

lives in western North Carolina with her husband, Doug, and her three boys, Douglas, Benjamin and Matthew. She began writing romances soon after Matthew was born. She's always wanted to write.

Elizabeth does counted cross-stitching to keep from eating at night. It doesn't always work. "I love to bowl, but I'm not very good. I keep my team's handicap high. I like hiking in the Shenandoahs, as long as we start up the mountain so the return trip is down rather than vice versa." She loves to go to Cape Hatteras to watch the sun rise over the ocean.

Elizabeth August has also published books under the pseudonym Betsy Page.

Dear Reader,

I am so excited to be a part of Silhouette Romance's CELEBRATION 1000! I can still remember the day I was first introduced to Romance novels. I have to confess, the daily stresses of life were getting me down. A friend said I needed something to relax me and she had the perfect solution. That night I read my first Romance novel. I was immediately hooked. The book had just what I was looking for: adventure, romance and most important, a happy ending. I became an avid reader.

Then came the day I sold my first book. That was one of the most exciting days of my life. This is a wonderful genre and I'm delighted to be a part of it. Even more, I am so very pleased to have this opportunity to express my appreciation to you, the romance readers. I owe you a debt of gratitude. Thank you so very much for allowing me to pursue a career that brings me such pleasure.

Best wishes,

Elizabeth August

Chapter One

The short-haired brunette lying in the hospital bed opened her eyes halfway. A throbbing headache was making it difficult for her to concentrate. As her vision cleared she saw there were two other people in the room. They were standing near the foot of her bed and even though they were talking in hushed tones, their voices were causing sharp bursts of pain.

One of the two was a very pretty, delicate-featured woman. Something over forty, the brunette guessed, judging the age from the faint lines the expertly applied makeup couldn't quite hide. The woman's blond hair was stylishly cut and her clothing, a deep purple silk suit, looked expensive in design. She was slender and average in height but carried herself with an air of authority that gave the impression she was used to being in command.

The other occupant of the room was a man. The brunette judged him to be in his early thirties. He was ruggedly handsome with a square cut chin and high cheekbones. His thick black hair was rumpled and the dark shadow of whiskers on his jaw was evidence he hadn't shaved recently. He was several inches taller than the woman and much larger in bulk. No flab, though, the brunette was sure. A curious curl of excitement twisted through her. The thought that he would be an adventure played through her mind. But not one I'd be wise in seeking, she added as she continued her inspection.

He was dressed in worn, grease-stained jeans and a sweatshirt that had seen better days. The sleeves of the sweatshirt had been ripped off and there was a tattoo of a snake wrapped around a knife on his upper arm. Definitely not a family man, she mused and was surprised by an unexpectedly sharp jab of regret.

The older woman and the man were obviously arguing. It took the brunette a moment before she could focus in on their words. When she did, she frowned.

"I knew something like this would happen when Eloise married you," the blonde was saying. Her voice was accusatory and brittle toward the man. The brunette also sensed no sympathy behind the other woman's words for whoever this Eloise person was. Instead there was an "I told her so" flavor.

"If I could have, I would have prevented this. I had no idea she would do something so foolish. I'd give my right arm to be there in her place," the man replied harshly. He looked tired as if he'd spent a long night's vigil and there was an honesty in his voice that left no

doubt in the brunette's mind that he meant what he
said.

"Dr. Green tells me they don't know for sure if she
has sustained any brain damage," the older woman
continued. "If she's a vegetable, I'll make certain all
of her inheritance is tied up for her care. You won't see
a red cent."

"If she's suffered any harm, I'll make certain she
gets the best care possible," the man returned curtly.

The woman's threat had caused the man's expression to grow grimmer. He looks dangerous, the brunette thought.

As if to confirm her judgment, she was sure she saw
a flash of fear cross the woman's face. Almost immediately it was replaced by cynicism. "A noble senti-
ment from someone everyone in town knows married
my daughter for her money," the woman flung back.

The brunette found herself beginning to feel agi-
tated and the headache with which she'd woken grew
worse. She didn't want to hear any more of this debate. "Could you two please take your argument
elsewhere. I've got a terrible headache," she grumbled.

"Eloise!" The woman swung her attention to the
bed. The relief of someone who has just had an unwanted burden lifted from her shoulders showed on
her face. "You're conscious and you're cognizant.
Thank goodness."

The brunette scowled in confusion. "I'm sorry, but
I am not Eloise and I don't know who either of you
are. You've obviously gotten into the wrong room so
would you mind taking your discussion elsewhere."

Shock replaced the relief on the older woman's face. She cast an accusing glance at the man, then returned her attention to the bed.

The man had not seen the older woman's hostile look. Instead his full attention was focused on the brunette. "What do you mean, you're not Eloise?" he asked.

The intensity of his gaze shook the brunette. His eyes, so dark brown they were almost ebony, seemed to bore into her. But what truly rattled her was the depth of honest concern she read on his face. She did not understand why it should, but his show of compassion surprised her. "I'm..." she began, then stopped. She fought to discover a name. There was only blankness.

"I'll get Dr. Green," the blonde said, already heading for the door.

Panic began to creep through the brunette. "I can't remember who I am," she admitted in a voice barely above a whisper.

The man's expression became guarded. "Do you remember anything?"

"I don't know." Her fear increasing, she concentrated harder. A vague image began to form in her mind. "I remember fishing. There was a pond." She closed her eyes and tried to concentrate but the headache was making thinking difficult. "It's a farm. I'm on a farm." She fought to make the image sharper. "I'm young, very young."

"The farm belonged to your father. It's yours now," the man said encouragingly.

"My father?"

"Lester Orman," the man elaborated. "He died several years ago."

"Lester Orman," the brunette repeated. The name conjured up an image of a tall, wiry man. He was balding and his skin was tanned as if he spent a lot of time in the sun. He was in what looked like a workshop intently concentrating on something on the bench in front of him. "My father," she said, experiencing a pang of sadness.

The door suddenly opened and a tall, thin elderly man wearing a doctor's coat entered. The woman who had been in the room before followed behind.

"Muriel tells me you seem to be having a little memory loss," the elderly man said, a friendly, encouraging smile on his face as he approached the bed.

"More than a little," the brunette replied, her fear again showing on her face.

"Now, don't you worry," he soothed, pulling out a light and flashing it in her eyes. "We had to do a little surgery to relieve the pressure. The trauma is probably causing a bit of short-term memory loss. You just relax."

His confident air gave the brunette hope and she drew a steadying breath.

"Now the two of you shoo," the doctor ordered, looking first at the man in the sweatshirt and then the purple-suited woman. "I need to examine my patient."

"What happened to me?" the brunette asked as soon as the others were gone. "How'd I get here?"

"You had a motorcycle accident. As I understand it from those who were there, you tried to do a wheelie and the bike threw you. You landed on your head. Luckily, as I've always said, you have one heck of a thick skull."

"You've known me a long time?" She concentrated hard on the age-lined face of the doctor but no memories stirred.

He finished counting her pulse before answering, then said, "I delivered you."

The brunette squeezed her eyes tightly shut trying even harder to dredge up a memory. Only shadowy images played through her mind. She groaned in frustration. "I can't remember."

"Getting yourself upset isn't going to help," he cautioned gently.

Recalling the conversation she'd heard when she'd first woken, her eyes popped open. An uneasiness stirred within her. "Then I am Eloise and I'm married to that man who was in here."

The doctor smiled with relief. "You remember that?"

"No, I heard the man and woman arguing when I woke up." Her gaze narrowed on him. "Who is the woman?"

"She's your mother."

"And she doesn't approve of my marriage," Eloise echoed the sentiments she'd heard expressed.

"Muriel is very conscious of her place in society," the doctor replied.

Eloise studied him. Her mother had implied the whole town disapproved of the man in the sweatshirt. She needed to know if this was so. "Do you approve of my marriage?"

"I delivered Jonah Tavish. He came into the world under difficult circumstances. You two aren't exactly a pair I would have matched up myself but your marriage appears to be working out just fine."

That wasn't what she'd call a strong vote of approval but it wasn't total disapproval, she noted. The brown-eyed man's image filled her mind. So his name was Jonah. From his dress and his manner she could have guessed he'd led a rough life and set his own rules. Judging from her memories of her father and the sight of her mother, she was certain her life had been very different. How had she ended up married to Jonah Tavish? she wondered.

Piercing pain shot through her head and exhaustion threatened to overwhelm her.

"I want you to stop trying to remember and just relax and rest," the doctor ordered. "You're going to be fine."

Deciding that taking his advice would be for the best, Eloise allowed herself to drift back to sleep.

Eloise sat propped up by pillows in her hospital bed. It was a little over three weeks since she'd first regained consciousness and she felt as if she was going to go crazy if she stayed there another day. She'd told Dr. Green this when he came by to check on her this morning. He'd informed her he'd allow her to leave with the restriction that she went home with either her husband or her mother.

"Not an easy choice," she muttered. She wasn't sure either really wanted her.

Her mother, she was certain, only came to visit out of a sense of duty. As for Jonah Tavish, he'd maintained a close vigil over her until he was certain she was on her way to recovering physically. After that, he'd continued to come every day to check on her. But his manner toward her was curiously noncommittal. He behaved more like a polite acquaintance than a husband. He'd never touched her or tried to kiss her.

She frowned as she admitted to herself that his attitude grated on her nerves. "It's not his attitude, it's me," she corrected under her breath. Whenever he entered her room she experienced a spark of excitement and found herself wondering how it would feel if he kissed her. Well, he is moderately good-looking and I'm not dead, she reasoned. Her frown deepened. "However, if he did marry me for my money, he must be having serious second thoughts about that decision," she concluded.

"Talking to yourself is a sure sign it's time you were getting out of here," Olivia Miller said, entering the room.

Eloise smiled at the nurse. During the past couple of weeks, she'd learned that Olivia was in her forties, had a husband of twenty-five years named Dan and four children. She'd also learned that, although this hospital was in Asheville, North Carolina, Olivia had been born and raised in Hornsburg, North Carolina. And Hornsburg, a little more than twenty miles southwest, nestled in the North Carolina mountains, was also where Eloise had been born and raised and was currently a resident. She'd merely been brought here because of the nature of her injury. "Do you know my husband?" Eloise asked bluntly.

"Hornsburg's a pretty small town and everyone sort of knows everyone else. Some folks I know better than others. As for your husband, it'd be fairer to say I know of him. Can't really say I know him," Olivia answered. "Now open," she ordered, getting ready to shove a thermometer into Eloise's mouth.

"What do you know *of* him?" Eloise managed to ask just before the instrument was inserted.

Olivia remained silent as she counted Eloise's pulse, then with a thoughtful expression, she said, "I know he's turned out a great deal better than a lot of people thought he would."

"How so?" Eloise asked around the glass rod under her tongue.

For a moment, Olivia hesitated, then she gave a shrug. "I can't see any harm in telling you. Dr. Green gave orders we're supposed to be giving you a chance to remember your past on your own. But it's not as if Jonah's childhood is any part of your memories. You two never really crossed each other's paths so's anyone would notice until you were all grown. Besides it'd probably be fairer to him if I told you about him than letting your mother give you her version of his past."

Eloise was certain the nurse was right on that point. If Jonah entered her room when her mother was visiting, Muriel's usual reaction was to grimace as if she'd just smelled something distasteful, bid her daughter a quick goodbye and leave. If Jonah was there when Muriel arrived, Muriel would not even enter the room. She'd simply say she'd be back later.

Olivia jotted down numbers on the chart she was holding, then returned her attention to Eloise.

Again Eloise saw hesitation on the nurse's face. "I have to make some important decisions," she said, trying to pronounce her words distinctly in spite of the thermometer. "I really need some information."

Olivia nodded as if to say this made sense. "I guess the politest way to describe Vivian Tavish, Jonah's mom, would be to say she was the unsettled type. She was seventeen and unwed when he was born. The man, Kirt Kagan, she claimed was his dad was barely nineteen. Kirt's family refused to have anything to do with the baby and Kirt took off for California before Vivian even brought Jonah home from the hospital. As far as I know, Jonah has never had any contact with the Kagans. Kirt never came back. The rest of the family ignored Jonah's existence. Now, Kirt's brothers and sisters have all left town and his parents moved to Florida several years ago."

Olivia paused to shake her head as if she didn't think the Kagans had behaved rightly, then continued, "Vivian's mom and dad volunteered to help raise the boy but it was more out of duty than love, I think. They always struck me as being real cold fish." An uneasiness showed in the nurse's eyes. Abruptly she glanced at her watch. "Time to check your temperature." Taking the thermometer out of Eloise's mouth, she read it. "Normal," she said with a smile.

Watching her, Eloise was sure the smile was strained. Clearly the nurse was uncomfortable about telling more regarding Jonah's history. Considering his coolness toward her, she'd be smart to simply let him stay erased from her memory, Eloise told herself. But her curiosity about the silent, grim man was too strong. "So he was raised by his mother and his grandparents?" she prodded as Olivia jotted down her temperature.

"Not exactly."

"How exactly was he raised?" Eloise persisted, her desire to know having grown so strong she was considering attempting to block the nurse's retreat if the woman tried to leave.

"His mom couldn't stand living with her parents," Olivia replied slowly. "I guess I can't blame her. They were pretty overbearing. From what I heard, they refused to allow her any freedom. She couldn't have friends in and they'd only take care of the baby when she was at work. All the rest of the time, they insisted she remain home and care for the child herself. It couldn't have been much of a life. It was more like an endless punishment for making a wrong decision."

Olivia sighed sympathetically. "Anyway, when Jonah was barely a year old, Vivian moved out on her own with the boy. She managed to keep clothes on their backs and food on the table."

"She sounds like a determined, valiant woman," Eloise said, wondering what was causing the curt edge in Olivia's voice.

A look of indecision played across the nurse's features, then her jaw tensed with purpose. "I think she just liked her freedom," she said bluntly. "Vivian was never one to let anyone tie her down. She took Jonah with her because her parents wouldn't keep him. She never married. She preferred to just live with her boyfriends and, through the years, she had several. That made Jonah's younger life pretty unstable. I don't think he ever got the kind of love or guidance he should have had at home."

Listening to the nurse, Eloise could easily visualize her silent, grim-faced husband as a young, sullen boy headed for real trouble. She began to feel very nervous about Jonah Tavish and wondered if her mother didn't have a right to be angry with her for marrying him. "But you mentioned you thought he'd turned out all right," she said, hoping the nurse had good reason to believe this.

Olivia smiled genuinely this time. "It was Clyde Gilder who turned the boy around. No one knows why but he took Jonah under his wing. Clyde owned the gas station a couple of blocks from where Jonah lived and he was considered the best mechanic for miles. He taught Jonah his craft."

"So my husband's a mechanic who works for Clyde Gilder," Eloise said, repeating the name so she'd remember it.

"Well, not exactly."

Eloise saw the uneasiness return to Olivia's face. "What exactly does my husband do for a living?" she asked bluntly.

"It's sort of a long story." The nervousness on Olivia's face intensified. "When he turned eighteen, Jonah got on his motorcycle and took off. People just assumed he wasn't coming back. His mother had gone down to Texas a year or so earlier with a rodeo rider and gotten herself bit by a rattlesnake, a sidewinder, I think. It was a big one and bit her a couple of times from what I heard. Anyway, she died. And Jonah and his grandparents hadn't spoken for years. So he didn't really have any blood ties that would bring him back here.

"Then about four years later, Clyde got sick. Jonah must have been keeping in touch with him because he came back and ran the garage for him. Clyde never got well enough to take over the business again. He was a widower and his only son had been killed over a decade earlier. He didn't have any close relatives he liked enough to mention in his will so when he died, no one was surprised to learn he'd left his garage and home to Jonah. Anyway, about a year ago it all burned down. They say the fire started in the garage but the house was so close and the fire was so hot, it caught and burned, too.''

''What is Jonah doing now?'' Eloise persisted, wondering if her husband was simply lying around her house living off her inheritance.

''You built him a new garage,'' Olivia replied, adding quickly, ''and he's made a real success of it. The man's a hard worker.'' Again, she abruptly glanced at her watch. ''Goodness! I'm running late,'' she blurted and hurried out of the room.

''So I built him his garage,'' Eloise murmured. The nurse's uneasiness and sudden departure told her something else. Olivia was among those who thought that Eloise's money was a primary reason for the marriage between her and Jonah Tavish. Eloise frowned. This was not a flattering image of herself or her marriage.

Wryly she wondered how Jonah had wooed her. Had she been so desperate for a husband she'd been willing to settle for the first man who asked? Or had he swept her off her feet? This last didn't really seem probable. Just trying to picture him smiling was difficult. Of course there was that sense of excitement she felt when he was in the room.

And she had seen a look of genuine concern on his face when she'd first woken. Also, to her surprise, he'd brought her flowers once. But still he'd kept his distance.

"Obviously, even though I must have felt at least some physical attraction toward him, he doesn't have any strong feelings toward me," she muttered.

A sharp knock jerked her attention to the door and she saw her mother enter.

"Dr. Green feels it's time for you to go home," Muriel said, approaching the bed.

Her mother looked more tense than usual, Eloise observed. Until this moment, she'd assumed she would have a choice of either going home with her husband or Muriel. Now suddenly it occurred to her that Muriel might not invite her. Aloud she said, "I'm glad because I'll go stir-crazy if I stay here another day."

Muriel nodded her understanding then her jaw firmed. "I'd take you home with me but you and Sidney have never hit it off."

I might not be able to remember any details but my instincts seem to be functioning just fine, Eloise thought, congratulating herself for guessing right about not being invited to convalesce at her mother's home.

Of course this hadn't been a totally instinctual guess, she admitted. She had managed to learn that her parents had been divorced when she was a toddler and that Sidney was her stepfather. He was a wealthy banker and land developer. She'd also learned she had two halfbrothers, Sidney, Jr. and Philip. The fact that neither of them nor their father had come to the hospital to visit her had given her the definite impression she was considered the black sheep in their family.

Still, it hurt to know her mother could so easily turn away from her. A question that had been nagging at the back of Eloise's mind again came to the forefront. She was pretty sure she'd get an answer she didn't want to hear but the question insisted on being asked. "Did you hate my father so much, that hatred has caused you to dislike me?"

Muriel frowned. "I don't dislike you."

"You don't seem to like me very much, either," she returned, determined to pursue this now that she'd broached the subject.

Muriel regarded her thoughtfully. "It's not that I don't like you, it's just that I wasn't ready to have a child."

"And because you weren't 'ready' to have a child, you couldn't find any love in your heart for me?" Eloise asked curtly.

Muriel frowned at the accusation in her daughter's voice. "I realize you don't remember, but we've had this conversation before. You and I have always been candid with one another. I see no reason to change that now."

She paused for a moment as if collecting her thoughts, then continued, "I married your father to make a better life for myself. My parents had no money and there were nine of us kids. I was lucky to have shoes to wear to school in the winter. I wanted a ticket out of there and marriage to Lester was it. His farm was bigger than the one my parents owned and there was just the two of us. I thought life would be better. And in a way it was.''

She frowned down at her carefully manicured fingernails, then returned her attention to her daughter. ''There was a little more money, and he was kind and good to me. But his inventions and his farm meant much more to him than I ever could. Besides, being a farmer's wife wasn't the life I was looking for anyway. You were an accident. I did my best to take care of you but all the time I was washing dirty diapers, I was wishing for a different kind of life-style.''

''And I was a stone around your neck,'' Eloise said dryly, wondering if she'd been drawn to Jonah because they both had mothers who didn't seem to care for them.

''No. I didn't think of you exactly like that. You and I just never seemed to quite fit together. You were sweet but quiet like your father. You even looked more like him than you did me. And you seemed to share more of a bond with him than you did with me. Then Sidney came back to town. He and I had been an item in our early years of high school but his family hadn't thought I was worthy of him. We discovered our earlier attraction hadn't disappeared. It had, in fact, grown stronger. I asked your father for a divorce and he gave me one without an argument.''

Apology showed on Muriel's face. ''I did take you with me. It seemed like the right thing to do. But from the first, Sidney was jealous. He didn't like being reminded that I'd ever been with another man. Your father and I decided you would be happier with your daddy.''

The apology was replaced with an expression of conviction. "And that arrangement clearly worked out for the best. You were happy with Lester. I'll admit he was very wrapped up in his work but that served to force you to learn to be independent and self-reliant. And I was able to have the life I wanted as well. It might not have been the most conventional solution but it was the most practical and worked out well for all of us."

A shadow of envy crossed Muriel's face. "It certainly turned out well for you. One of your father's inventions actually proved to be useful and made you a very wealthy woman."

"So it seems," Eloise replied, mentally making a note to find out as soon as possible just how much she was worth. She also found herself wondering what she'd thought as a child when her mother had sent her back to her father. Had she understood or had she felt abandoned? Considering the fact that her stepfather's attitude toward her must have made her feel disliked and uncomfortable in his home, she decided she must have experienced some of both emotions. And that was, she admitted, how she was feeling at this moment. However, there was also a mingling of relief as if down deep inside she knew her place was not with her mother.

"Now it's time for you to go home," Muriel repeated, returning the conversation to its original subject. "And the doctor feels you should be where you'll be the most comfortable. That will be your farm. After your father struck it rich, he had the place remodeled and enlarged. And, through the years, you've had work done on it." Muriel shifted uneasily. "Jonah will be there, of course, after all he is your husband. However, he has assured me he won't make any demands on you and the place is large and spacious enough that you can have as much privacy as you want." Her jaw firmed again. "Also, I've arranged for your aunt Sarah to come stay with you, too. She's a trained nurse. Luckily she was available. She'll be perfect."

Eloise frowned. "Aunt Sarah? Until just now, when you mentioned brothers and sisters, I was under the impression you were the only family I had," she said, wondering if all her aunts and uncles lived a goodly distance away or if they hadn't come to visit or sent cards because they, too, considered her a black sheep.

"No. There are more," Muriel admitted. "Your father had several brothers and sisters as well. But none of his family live around here. They're scattered all over the world. I believe you correspond with some or all of them on occasion, but I wasn't particularly fond of any of them. Since the divorce, I've had very little contact with that side of your family." She gave a little shrug of dismissal as if to say her late husband's family was of little importance, then continued coolly, "As for my family, we're not close. My brothers and sisters have their own lives to lead."

The indifference in her mother's voice let Eloise know Muriel felt no family ties with any of her siblings. It would seem that Sidney and her sons are the only ones my mother really cares for, Eloise mused. No wonder she couldn't remember any of her past, she added dryly. She had a mother who didn't want her and a husband who only wanted her for her money. And now she was going to be subjected to an aunt who probably didn't want to bother with her, either. "But, in spite of her busy life, you've convinced your sister to come look after me," she said sarcastically.

"Definitely not! I'm your late father's sister!" a voice boomed from the doorway. "And I didn't need any convincing to come."

Eloise saw her mother flinch. Looking past Muriel, her attention was first caught by a brightly colored floral dress. It hung with a comfortable looseness upon a tall, trim figure. Her gaze shifted to the face of the woman who had spoken. She guessed the new-comer's age to be somewhere around forty. The woman's features were sharply defined and her ebony hair, very lightly peppered with gray, was braided and wound tightly around her head in a severe style.

A fleeting moment of familiarity swept through her as she noticed the woman had the same gray eyes as herself. Then it was gone and her gaze shifted back to the dress. The cheeriness of its colors and design seemed incongruent with the staid facial appearance of the newcomer. Eloise's attention traveled to the shoes. They were bright red, matching some of the flowers in the dress as well as the woman's purse.

"I came as soon as I heard what had happened," Sarah continued, striding to the bed. "Muriel didn't contact me until yesterday." She cast Muriel an accu-satory glance. "She didn't contact any of us."

"I didn't see any reason to worry you or your fam-ily unnecessarily," Muriel returned defensively.

Watching the exchange, Eloise realized her mother was intimidated by this new arrival. She'd been under the impression no one could intimidate Muriel and she found this interesting. Then Aunt Sarah turned her gaze to her and she understood how her mother felt.

"I can't believe my so very proper, so very tame, so very, very conventional niece has gotten herself into this muddle." Sarah's expression stern, she added solemnly, "An ounce of prevention is worth a pound of cure." Then unexpectedly, she grinned and her eyes suddenly gleamed with mischief. "Doing a wheelie on Main Street in front of the populus, no less. Good heavens, it was a foolish thing to do but I wish I could have seen it."

Eloise found herself smiling back, a crooked self-conscious smile.

"I'll leave you two to get reacquainted," Muriel interjected. "I'm due at a charity function." Pausing only for a moment, she gave Eloise's cheek a light brush of a kiss, then with a wave to both her daughter and former sister-in-law she left hastily.

Sarah's expression again became dour as she watched the departure. When she returned her attention to Eloise, her manner was businesslike. "But enough about wheelies, now it's time to get you back to your old self."

"Maybe I didn't like my old self." Eloise flushed when she realized what she'd just said. But this thought had been plaguing her and she finished it aloud. "Maybe that's why I can't remember anything."

"No one's perfect," Sarah replied with equal bluntness. "And no one I've ever known has ever been completely satisfied with their lives. But I've never thought of you as someone who'd run away just because life got a little difficult. You've always been the 'when life knocks you down, you get up and punch it in the nose' kind of person. I'm certain you can't remember because you bruised your brain and as soon as it's had a little time to heal your memory will come back."

The woman spoke with such authority Eloise could almost believe her. A wave of apprehension swept through her. The thought that maybe it would be best if she simply didn't remember flashed through her mind. But she knew she had to try.

Chapter Two

Eloise sat in the front seat of the gray BMW. Jonah was driving and Aunt Sarah had fallen asleep in the back.

Covertly Eloise studied her husband. The second time she'd woken in the hospital, he'd been there, clean-shaven and dressed in a fresh cotton shirt with a button-down collar and jeans that had seen better days but were clean. From that day to this, that had been his usual attire. However, as her gaze traveled down his leg to the heavy black biker's boots, the image of how he'd looked that first time she'd woken came vividly to her mind. She saw him with the dark stubble giving his already grim expression an added harshness. Then there was the grease-smeared sweatshirt, the dusty jeans, the tattoo on his arm and the long, thin white scar on the left side of his face.

She also recalled all that Olivia had told her and the thought that he might have ridden with a motorcycle gang during those years he was gone crossed her mind. I should be wary of him, she thought. He did make her nervous and edgy. But an examination of her feelings revealed this wasn't due to fear. What bothered her was how much he interested her. In fact, she was forced to admit, when he was around she found it difficult to pull her attention away from him. And her instincts seemed to be warning her this was a dangerous preoccupation.

"My aunt said she'd just flown in this morning. Guess the trip wore her out," she said, unable to continue bearing the silence that had filled the vehicle since they'd left the hospital.

"She came in from Australia. It's my guess she's going to be catnapping for a few days until her body rhythm gets accustomed to our time zone again," he replied.

His tone was polite but cool and she noted his jaw was set in a hard line. "I hope you don't mind her coming to stay with us." She wasn't sure why she was apologizing but it seemed like the right thing to do.

Anger suddenly shadowed his features. "You don't need any protection from me. I promised your mother I'd treat you fairly and I will." The anger vanished as quickly as it had come and again his expression became unreadable. "However, I don't mind having Sarah around. She can be disconcertingly blunt at times but a person always knows where they stand with her."

Eloise thought she caught a hint of accusation in his voice. A realization that had been nagging at her again forced itself to the forefront. Although he'd visited her on a regular basis, they'd never had what could be termed a personal exchange. They'd talked about the weather and he'd asked her how she felt, but it was as if both had steered away from any intimate conversation. *I may never get my memory back and there are things I need to know,* she told herself. Aloud, she asked, "Didn't you always know where you stood with me?"

"Sometimes I thought I did. Sometimes I wasn't sure," he replied, his attention remaining on the road. A cynical smile suddenly played at one corner of his mouth. "But then I suppose most relationships with men and women are ambiguous at best."

The temptation to ask him to define what their relationship had been was strong, but the words stuck in her throat. The thought that she was afraid of what he might say shook her. *I'm just not ready for too many personal revelations,* she countered. Besides, how could she know if he was telling her the truth? Better to wait a little, she decided.

Again a silence fell between them and Eloise felt her tension return. She was on her way to a farm to live with two people who were, for all practical purposes, total strangers. Again attempting to relieve her nervousness with conversation, she searched for a safe subject. "Nice car," she heard herself saying.

"It's yours," Jonah returned with cool indifference. "I figured you and your aunt would be more comfortable in it than in my old pickup."

Eloise glanced around at the plush leather upholstery. The interior of the car reeked of wealth. She frowned. In addition to avoiding asking about her and

Jonah's relationship, she'd also avoided attempting to pry anything about herself from him. And her success with others in this endeavor had proved less than satisfactory.

The pond and her father was all she'd remembered of her past and even that was vague. Aunt Sarah had referred to her as being conventional and proper. Yet she'd married a man who looked like a biker and was grimmer than death. And she'd gotten her injury attempting to do a wheelie in front of a town full of people. It was actually a small gathering in front of Jonah's garage, she corrected, trying to limit her sense of embarrassment. Deciding that attempting to subtly extract information from Jonah would prove to be a waste of time, she asked bluntly, "How did I spend my days? Was I one of the idle rich?"

This time he did glance toward her and she was almost sure she saw a flash of admiration in his eyes. Then again his expression became unreadable. Turning his attention back to the road, he said, "There was never anything idle about you. You have a degree in Business Administration and you're a Certified Public Accountant. When you graduated from college you bought into a partnership with Paul Thompson. You and he have a very profitable accounting business."

"Paul Thompson. He was one of the four people other than my mother and you who came to see me." The image of a short, plump, father-acting man, who looked to be in his early fifties, maybe older, filled her mind. He'd been nearly completely bald and worn glasses so thick, she'd barely been able to see his eyes. "He said he was a business associate but he didn't elaborate. I thought maybe he simply managed my money for me."

"Because of those headaches you were having until just a couple of days ago, Doc Green kept your visitors at a minimum. He also wanted your memories to be your own and not something implanted by someone else so he gave whoever came strict instructions they were not to talk about their relationship to you. They were only there to see if their faces and names would trigger any recall on your part."

Eloise nodded. "I remember the rules." It also dawned on her that, without any coercion from her, Jonah had just broken them. "Since you're actually answering my questions about myself, can I assume the rules have changed?"

"Doc agrees that it's time for you to get on with your life. Your headaches have subsided, so he feels you can deal with being given more information."

"Besides, my memory might not return and I can't live in a state of limbo forever," she interjected, letting him know she fully understood all the possibilities.

His frown deepening, Jonah nodded.

Her appetite whetted, Eloise recalled the faces of the others who had come. There had been a Reverend Randal, a youngish man, pleasant face, full head of dark brown hair that threatened to be unruly, brown eyes and a nice smile. "Was I active in my church?"

"You attended regularly."

Pushing aside the image of the reverend, she thought of the middle-aged, small, slender woman, with dark brown hair and hazel eyes, dressed in a conservative gray suit. The woman had introduced herself as Mary Howe and she'd had a motherly smile.

"Mary Howe said she was my secretary. Is she my social secretary or what?"

"She works at the accounting firm. You lived a pretty ordinary life and had no reason for a social secretary."

She glanced out the window, considering the portrait of herself that Jonah had sketched out. Other than choosing the taciturn man beside her for a husband, she did seem to have followed a very conservative life-style.

Her fourth visitor came to mind. Charles Polaski had been, she judged, in his late fifties or early sixties. He was a slender man, somewhere near six feet tall and dressed in a tailored three-piece suit. His manner had been polite but businesslike. He'd informed her he was her attorney and had been her father's attorney and friend. And he'd advised her to seek him out before signing anything.

Thinking about the lawyer, she recalled that while her other visitors had shown open concern and sympathy, there had been a professional coolness in Mr. Polaski's manner. Admittedly he'd expressed concern for her and she'd felt it was genuine, still she'd had the distinct impression they were more business acquaintances than friends. "Do I trust Mr. Polaski?" she asked.

"As far as I know, you do," Jonah replied. "He and his son have always handled you and your father's business and personal affairs."

Eloise studied the man beside her. "Do you trust him?"

"Yes," Jonah replied.

It was curious, she thought, that she'd sought her husband's judgment on the character of her lawyer. This observation was quickly followed by the realization that her instinct was to trust Jonah's opinion. Frustration swept through her. She wanted to remember what their marriage had been like.

She drew a terse breath as a sharp pain shot through her head. Trying too hard to break down whatever barrier was surrounding her memory would only give her a monster of a headache. This she knew from experience. Concentrate on what you've just learned, she ordered herself.

"So I'm a career woman," she mused. Her gaze traveled along the taut line of Jonah's jaw and, in spite of her command to herself, she continued to wonder about their marriage. "How could a conservative, successful businesswoman get herself into this situation?" she muttered, then flushed when she realized she'd spoken aloud.

"I wouldn't know," he replied crisply.

Another thought occurred to her. She'd gone this far, she might as well ask, she reasoned. "Do I have a wild side nobody is telling me about?"

He grinned abruptly as if this question was so amusing he could not keep himself from smiling. "Not that I know of." As quickly as it had appeared, the grin vanished and an expression of reprimand took its place. "Of course that wheelie was out of character. You weren't ready to try that yet and you knew it."

Eloise barely noticed this last statement. His smile had stunned her. She thought she'd never seen a man look more attractive. He had two long dimples and there had been a softening of his features that had actually made him appear approachable. "You can smile." Again she'd spoken without thinking and again she flushed.

He cocked an eyebrow in her direction as if to say he found her observation trivial.

"Well, this is the first time I can remember ever seeing you smile," she returned in her defense. "I was beginning to think your muscles refused to function in that manner."

"My muscles perform just fine in every manner," he returned curtly.

An unexpected surge of heat raced through her. For one brief instant, she saw herself in his arms. They were in bed, tangled in a lovers' embrace. She was laughing as he nuzzled her neck. A fire ignited within her. Then the image was gone, leaving her shaken. "I'm sure they do," she replied.

Covertly she studied the man beside her as another silence descended over the car. Had they really been such hot lovers or was her imagination working overtime? Now that's a question I'm definitely not ready to ask yet, she decided.

"Do I have a domestic side?" she asked instead.

"You've never seemed to mind housework but you do have Nancy Perkins come in and clean once a week." He paused, then added, "You're a good cook."

She'd noticed his hesitation before offering this opinion and wondered what had caused it. "I am?"

"It was a surprise to me," he responded in answer to the skepticism in her voice.

Eloise was considering what to ask next when he flicked on his turn signal and slowed. She'd been concentrating so hard on him, she hadn't been aware of how long they'd been driving. Now she realized they'd left Asheville behind ages ago. For a while they'd been on a dual-lane highway but for the past several miles they'd been traveling along a sharply winding two-lane road. To her right was bottomland skirting a river. A healthy crop of corn was beginning to sprout in the fertile soil. Across the river she saw huge round bales of hay dotting a newly harvested field.

To her left the land was untamed, mountainous, sloping sharply upward. Cutting into this wilderness was a gravel road with a sign stating this was a private driveway. It was onto this road that Jonah turned. As he guided the car along the steep, winding roadway, she realized she hadn't seen a house in quite a while. For some distance, they drove through thickly wooded terrain, then emerged into an area where a wide swath of the land to her left had been cleared creating a meadow. The meadow was fenced and on it four horses grazed lazily. Beyond that was a well-kept stable. To her right she saw a two-story farmhouse. Her nerves tensed further. "Is this where we live? How far does our land extend? Is there a neighbor over the ridge?" she asked all in a rush, a part of her hoping to discover there was someone else nearby.

"*You* own this place," he corrected. "You used to own a great deal more land, but after your father died, you sold most of it and just kept the forty-eight acres surrounding the house."

Her gaze raked over the landscape. "Do I raise any crops?"

"No. You sold the good farming land. What you kept is pretty rough terrain and rocky."

"I suppose no one wanted to buy it," she speculated, a part of her awed by the beauty of the land while another was struck by the isolation.

"Rumor was you had a good offer to sell it to a developer for homesites but you kept it to have space to ride your horses," he replied, parking in front of the well-maintained house fronted by a garden of wildflowers.

Eloise looked back at the horses grazing in the meadow. Instinctively, she knew she would be comfortable with them. "What was I doing on a motorcycle instead of a horse?" she muttered.

Jonah's gaze leveled on her. "A couple of months ago, you decided to give motorcycles a try."

Eloise frowned. "That was obviously a mistake."

"Obviously," he agreed.

A frigid edge in his voice caused her to feel as if she'd insulted him. "I have nothing against motorcycles," she said quickly. "But they are clearly not for me. I guess a person should stick to what suits them best."

"That would be safer and wiser," he confirmed.

She saw the icy cynicism in his eyes before his expression again became shuttered. She was not certain how, but she knew she'd just thickened the barrier between them.

"Time to get you settled into your home once again," Aunt Sarah's voice abruptly cut into Eloise's thoughts. "Home is where the heart is and that's the best place to be when you're in need of healing."

Surprised to have forgotten about the woman, Eloise glanced over her shoulder to see Sarah climbing out of the back. Her aunt, she noted, seemed to have an adage for every occasion.. And she fervently hoped Sarah was right about this being a healing place. She reached for the door handle, but Sarah was already there opening the door for her. The moment Eloise was standing, Sarah took her by the arm and guided her toward the house.

Frustration swept through Eloise. She'd hoped to experience a sense of homecoming upon her arrival here. Instead she simply felt nervous as she mounted the short flight of steps to the front porch.

Jonah had been walking behind the women carrying the small suitcase packed with a few of Eloise's belongings he'd brought to the hospital. As the women reached the door, he stepped in front of them, unlocked the door, then stepped aside to allow them to enter before him.

Eloise paused in the entrance foyer. There was a familiarity about this place. "Was I really happy here?" The question burst out before she even realized the words had formed in her mind.

"Obviously not recently," Jonah replied, his gaze cool and impersonal as it met hers.

"Now let's not go jumping to any conclusions," Sarah interjected forcefully. Slipping her arm around Eloise's waist, she guided her toward the stairs. "We need to get you settled in and once I've got some good home cooking into you, I'm sure you'll feel more cheerful."

The sudden image of herself as a young girl sitting down at the kitchen table and staring at a bean-and-rice casserole topped with melted marshmallows and smelling strongly of brown sugar, cinnamon and nutmeg suddenly filled Eloise's mind. In front of her was a teenage version of Sarah, clothed in jeans and a pale pink blouse, her black hair hanging freely down her back, loosely held away from her face with a matching pink ribbon. "I created this especially for you," the young version of Sarah was saying, smiling with pride.

The image broadened and Eloise realized her father was at the table also. "Heaven save us all from Sarah's creations in the kitchen," he muttered for Eloise's ears only.

As this flash of memory vanished as quickly as it had appeared, she started to say she wasn't really hungry, but the sentence stuck in her throat. She didn't want to insult her aunt. If Sarah left, Eloise would be alone with Jonah and she wasn't ready for that. Besides, she was already beginning to like her.

Sarah turned to Jonah. "You show Eloise to her room." As she spoke, she released her hold on Eloise's arm then lifted Eloise's hand and placed it on Jonah's arm.

Eloise bit back a gasp of surprise as the contact sent a rush of warmth through her. Beneath her palm she felt Jonah's muscles tense. She glanced up at his face to see an impatience shadowing his features and instantly felt like a nuisance. "I'm sure I can navigate the stairs on my own," she said, quickly releasing his arm.

Sarah scowled and immediately returned Eloise's hand to Jonah's arm. "I will not have you getting dizzy and falling and hitting your head again," she said. "You've been lying around for better than three weeks now. Your muscles are bound to be a little unsteady."

Jonah's jaw firmed. "Sarah's right."

Before Eloise could react, he'd freed his arm from her light touch and gripped her just above the elbow. The strength of his fingers sent a ripple of excitement through her and again the image of being in his embrace raced through her mind. Then she saw the ice in his eyes and a coolness descended over her. Although she'd clearly been attracted to him, she had her doubts about him ever being truly attracted to her. Pride caused her back to stiffen. Wanting only to be free of his touch as quickly as possible, she started up the stairs without further protest.

She expected him to release her when they reached the landing. Instead he continued to hold on to her as he guided her down the hall to her right and into the first room on her left. Only when she was inside did he free her.

Setting her suitcase on the floor by the bed, he said, "I've moved my things into the guest room at the other end of the hall." Straightening, his cool gaze leveled on her. "I want you to know that you're not shackled to me."

A possible explanation for her memory block occurred to her. "Was I feeling trapped in our marriage?" she asked bluntly.

"You never actually said so but there'd been a growing tension between us. Maybe if I'd left earlier, this accident would never have happened." His jaw set in a firm line. "But I figure right now you need someone to help watch over you. So, I'll stay until I know you're going to be all right, then I'm going to move on."

"I'm sorry I can't remember about us," she said, feeling the need to apologize. Again the image of being in his arms flashed into her mind but she chose not to mention that. She was not willing to judge their relationship on a single brief remembered moment of passion. Besides, considering the distance he was keeping between them, she was still finding it difficult to believe this memory was real.

He shrugged. "Even we didn't really expect our marriage to last."

Eloise studied him narrowly. "We didn't?"

"We're cut from different cloths and we knew it," he replied, then abruptly left.

Listening to his heavy booted footsteps going down the hall, she knew he was right. "Maybe I can't remember anything because I just want a fresh start," she murmured, then headed into the bathroom to take a warm shower.

Chapter Three

Eloise frowned grumpily at her image in the mirror. The shower she'd hoped would help her relax hadn't. And her hair wasn't helping her mood, she admitted as she dried the brown tresses. On one side they were thick, long, extending a little below her shoulder, and wavy. On the other, where her hair had been shaved for the operation, she was still in what she considered the stubble stage. "It sort of looks like one of those mod hairstyles," she mused.

Abruptly she found herself wondering if Jonah had known other women with hair cut in unusual styles on purpose and maybe tattoos on their arms or in more private places. A small knot that felt like jealousy formed in her stomach.

Irritation toward herself etched itself into her features. "He and I don't have anything in common. Our marriage had to have been based on a physical attraction…and from his reactions to me, it's my guess the attraction was mine not his.''

A coldness spread through her. Then a fresh thought jolted her. Had she been so enamored of him she'd gotten a tattoo herself? Quickly she discarded the towel she'd wrapped around herself and made a thorough inspection.

"No tattoos," she breathed with a sigh of relief.

Refastening the towel around her torso, she turned her attention to her face. She had a pleasant enough appearance, she decided. However, unlike her mother who was delicately beautiful, she was rather average and with a slightly larger bone structure. Her lips were full, her face more rounded and her nose shorter and broader. "I obviously do take after my father's side of the family," she concluded, recalling that her gray eyes matched Sarah's both in shade and shape.

Giving a shrug as if to say that what she looked like was the least of her worries at the moment, she headed into the bedroom. The bathroom was private, opening only into the bedroom. Because of that, she'd expected her privacy to be insured. Next time I'll remember to lock the door, she thought as her gaze locked with Jonah's and she froze in midstride.

Easing his long form out of the upholstered chair by the window, he said coolly, "I heard the water running. When I realized you were taking a shower, I thought I should stick around and make sure you didn't get dizzy and fall and hurt yourself."

His manner was businesslike, reminding her of someone performing a duty they were not pleased to find on their shoulders. Anger flared. Again he'd made her feel like a nuisance. "I really don't need you to watch over..." she began, her voice matching his in coldness. But the end of the sentence died in her throat as his gaze raked over her and the brown of his eyes darkened. The ice that had been in those brown depths was replaced by a desire so intense that even across the distance separating them she could feel the heat.

"Looks like you're doing fine on your own," he growled, and stalked out of the room.

Shaken, she stood staring at the door as it swung closed behind him. Apparently the physical attraction between them hadn't been entirely one-sided. "Or maybe he's just been without a woman long enough any warm body would spark a fire," she rebutted, determined not to jump to any conclusions. After all, until a moment ago she'd been certain he held no feelings for her.

"Besides, I'm sure lust isn't a good foundation for a marriage," she added, although it did appear that at one time she'd been willing to settle for just that.

But as hard as she tried to put that heated look in his eyes out of her mind, it taunted her. Too restless to hide out in her room, she began searching for clothes. The first door she opened was to an empty walk-in closet.

"When Jonah said he'd moved out, he meant he'd *moved out,*" she muttered, reason telling her this must have been his closet. She expected to feel relieved. Instead a pang of hurt pierced her.

"I wish I could remember," she groaned in frustration, pulling the door shut. Her head started to pound and she forced herself to stop trying.

Striding to the next door, she opened it and discovered a second walk-in closet. This one was filled with women's clothes. "Mine," she said with assurance, again feeling a nudging of familiarity.

To her right were stylish suits, expensive-looking blouses and tailored slack outfits along with several dresses. Purses and matching pairs of shoes were neatly arranged on shelves on the wall beside the door. From the rack on the end wall hung a few cocktail dresses and two long formal gowns along with some dressy slacks and fancy tops.

To her left hung jeans, corduroy slacks, sweatshirts, T-shirts, along with less dressy button-down and pullover shirts, skirts, blouses and dresses. Arranged in a shoe rack on the wall, were a couple of pairs of sneakers, some very comfortable-looking shoes and sandals and several pairs of cowboy boots. On the shelf above were four Stetson hats, a brown one, a black one, a tan one and a white one. "A plethora of clothes," she murmured.

Choosing a pair of jeans, a sweatshirt and the sneakers, she dressed, then went downstairs.

At the foot of the stairs, she saw the dining room to her right and living room to her left. Her stomach growled, reminding her it was lunchtime. Assuming the kitchen would be somewhere in the vicinity of the dining room, she turned to her left. At the end of a corridor, she pushed open a door through which the odor of cooking was coming and discovered a huge country-style kitchen. Seated at a long, large wooden table in the center of the room was Jonah. He was staring dubiously at the plate of food in front of him.

"My concoctions always taste better than they look," Sarah was saying, frowning impatiently down at him. "You should also keep in mind that it's unwise to harass the cook unless you like lumpy oatmeal." Her gaze became even sterner. "I'd suggest you taste my food before you pass judgment."

He held up a hand as if in surrender. "I'm going to. I just have to work up my courage."

"I'd never have taken you for a comedian," Sarah snapped back.

Nor would I, Eloise thought, surprised by his show of dry humor. She'd begun to think he didn't have a sense of humor at all.

He forked a bite of what looked to be red scrambled eggs heavily dotted with something green.

"Well?" Sarah demanded, her tone daring him to say anything derogatory.

"They're interesting," he replied, diplomatically.

"Interesting is good enough," Sarah returned with an air of triumph.

At that moment, as if he sensed they were not alone, Jonah suddenly jerked his attention to the doorway in which Eloise was standing. The desire she'd seen in his eyes a little earlier was missing. There was only cool politeness. "Shouldn't you be resting?" he asked, a strong note of dismissal in his voice suggesting she should return to her room immediately.

"Yes, she should be," Sarah confirmed.

Eloise's back stiffened in defiance. Obviously I don't like taking orders, she realized. Aloud, she said firmly, "I've been lying around for weeks now. And I'm hungry."

"I was going to have Jonah bring a tray up to you as soon as he finished eating," Sarah replied, already heading back to the stove. "But as long as you're here you might as well join him. Sit," she ordered.

"Remember her stomach's been used to hospital food," Jonah cautioned, frowning at Sarah's back. "Maybe you should make her scrambled eggs plain."

Sarah tossed him an impatient glance. "She'll have them with tomato, onions and parsley just like yours. She needs variety as well as her protein."

Jonah cast Eloise a look that said "I tried" as she seated herself at the far end of the table. This small protective gesture caused her heart to skip a beat. Self-directed anger filled her. Only a short while ago he'd made it clear he had no deep feelings for her. I can't believe he can elicit such strong reactions from me over the smallest of kindnesses, she fumed silently.

"You'll seat yourself either next to Jonah or across from him," Sarah commanded over her shoulder. "I don't see any reason for me to walk any farther than necessary to deliver this food."

Admitting the man unnerved her, Eloise rebelled at being any closer to him than was absolutely necessary. "I can get my own food," she replied, rising and moving to the coffeepot.

"Makes me nervous having people underfoot," Sarah fussed. "I'll bring your food to you."

Knowing she would look like either a fool or a coward or both if she refused to cooperate, Eloise carried her coffee back to the table and eased into the chair opposite Jonah.

Anger showed on his face as he glanced up at her. "I don't bite," he said in a lowered voice as she took a sip of coffee.

The sudden image of him nibbling on her earlobe caused a heat to race through Eloise. Quickly she feinted an intense interest in her coffee.

"Of course he won't bite," Sarah affirmed, unexpectedly appearing at the table. She placed a bowl of what looked like brown grits in front of Eloise. "You can start on these while I cook your eggs. They contain plenty of carbohydrates and sugar for fast energy." Her gaze shifted to Jonah. "And you eat your eggs before they get cold."

"Yes, ma'am," he replied.

Eloise had glanced up. She again saw a flash of humor in Jonah's eyes in response to Sarah's bossy mothering. Then it was gone and his expression became shuttered as he returned his attention to his food. But just that one brief glimpse of boyish amusement remained vivid in her mind and caused a warm glow within her. The man doesn't want to be here. He married me for my money and nothing more, she reminded herself curtly. Stop thinking about him! she ordered and turned her attention to her food.

With her spoon poised, she hesitated. She was hungry enough to eat almost anything but she had real doubts about whatever this was in front of her.

"It's grits flavored with brown sugar, nutmeg and cinnamon." Jonah's lowered voice broke into her contemplations. "And it's not as bad as it looks."

"Thank you," Sarah called from the stove, letting him know she'd heard him.

Eloise's stomach growled again. Jonah obviously ate it and survived, she reasoned and spooned a bite into her mouth. Unusual but not bad, she decided and ate more.

"Now that you two are taken care of, I'm going to go have another little nap. My body's still on Australian time," Sarah announced as she placed the scrambled eggs and toast in front of Eloise. Her gaze rested on Jonah. "You said you put my things in the yellow guest room?"

"Up the stairs, turn left, first door on your left," he instructed.

Sarah nodded. "Same place it's always been."

Before Eloise could issue a polite thank-you for the eggs, her aunt was on her way out the kitchen door.

The moment Sarah was gone, Jonah rose, picked up the plate of eggs Sarah had just given Eloise, carried them to the sink and scraped them off.

Startled, she sat mutely watching as he got out more eggs and began scrambling them. "You actually seem to know what you're doing at that stove," she observed, trying not to think about how good he looked in a pair of jeans.

"I was on my own for a lot of years," he returned.

And soon to be again, Eloise thought, recalling his announcement that he would be leaving before long. Studying the hard set of his jaw, she could tell he was uncomfortable being there with her and wondered why he wasn't already packed. After all, she had Sarah to watch over her. Again he made her feel like a nuisance. "You don't have to wait on me," she said tightly. "I would have eaten my aunt's eggs. You did."

"My stomach is used to almost anything," he replied coolly, dishing up the eggs and adding two slices of whole wheat toast to the plate. Then setting the plate in front of her, he said, "If you think you'll be all right here with Sarah, I've got work waiting for me at the garage."

"I'll be fine," she replied with dismissal.

Nodding, he picked up his plate, rinsed it, put it into the dishwasher, then headed for the door. But as he started out of the room, he paused. "I've written the phone number for the garage and taped it by the phone. If you need anything, call me."

"Sure," she replied while mentally vowing she'd rather die than ask for his assistance. She was more certain than ever he didn't want to be there and again she wondered why he was sticking around.

He again started out the door, then paused and turned back once more. "And remember Doc Green said you've got to limit your activities for at least a couple more weeks so don't go trying to chase after those horses of yours. Jed Beeck's been looking after them for you for the past five years. He's totally reliable and they're doing just fine."

His ordering her around grated on her nerves but admitting to herself that she was not yet in shape to take care of any large beasts, she nodded her agreement.

This time he completed his exit, leaving her alone in the kitchen.

"And now I think it's time to find out more about myself starting with how much I'm worth," she muttered under her breath.

Glancing around the kitchen she spotted the phone. It was hanging on the wall and a shelf below it held a phone book along with a notepad and a mug full of pens and pencils. "I clearly ran an efficient household," she said with approval as she rose and strode across the room.

She found Charles Polanski's number and dialed. His secretary put her through to the lawyer immediately and he readily made an appointment to come out to the farm within the hour.

That business taken care of, she ate the eggs and toast because she was hungry. But even as she wolfed down the food, she promised herself she'd accept no more aid from Jonah Tavish. In fact, she might just pack his bags and have them waiting for him on the porch when he returned.

Eloise finished scanning the legal document, then looked up at her lawyer. "According to this prenuptial agreement, Jonah has no legal claim to any of my money whether our marriage remains intact or ends in divorce."

"That was at his insistence," Charles Polanski replied. "Originally you and I had worked out an agreement I felt was more than generous but he refused to sign it."

Eloise frowned in confusion. "I was so sure he married me for my money," she admitted bluntly.

Charles's staid manner became even more somber. "I'm not saying your money didn't have something to do with the marriage."

Eloise regarded him narrowly. "How exactly did my money come into it?"

"His garage and equipment had been old and out-dated. The insurance he carried on them was minimal. And he hadn't carried any insurance on the house. You gave him the funds to rebuild his business," Charles elaborated. "And you insisted on enlarging the enterprise and purchasing the very best equipment."

Understanding flashed in Eloise's eyes. So that was it! He'd gotten his profit up front.

"However," Charles continued. "He kept track of every cent that was spent and is paying you back on a monthly basis. He wanted to pay interest but you refused that."

"The man's an enigma," Eloise groaned, again at a loss for why Jonah was sticking around when she was sure he wanted to go his own way.

"When you came to me and told me of your intention to marry Jonah Tavish, I cautioned you to think twice," Charles said, a shadow of fatherly concern actually flickering across his features.

"Then you don't approve of my marriage?" she asked wondering if there was anyone who did.

"I had my misgivings," he continued soberly. "However, some marriages surprise people. Yours was one of those. The two of you seemed to bring out the best in each other." He frowned thoughtfully. "I'm not saying I think you had the perfect relationship. I sensed there was some tension at times but that's only natural."

I certainly don't seem to be bringing out the best in Jonah Tavish at the moment, Eloise thought, finding the lawyer's description of her marriage hard to reconcile with the way her husband was acting toward her. "So you honestly thought our marriage was working?" she asked skeptically.

"You came to see me two months ago and changed your will. You left the majority of your estate to Jonah and any children the two of you might bear."

Eloise stared at the man. "I was talking about bearing his children?" She had to admit, she'd had a few erotic reactions to the man, but bearing his children was another matter entirely.

Charles's gaze leveled on her. "I've known you from the day you were born. You've never been a frivolous woman. You have, in the view of some, been much too serious even as a child. And you've always been very firm about never bringing children into a marriage where they would not be welcomed. In fact it was the mention of the offspring that convinced me a new will was appropriate."

A little later as Eloise stood on her front porch watching the lawyer drive away, she was still having a difficult time believing she'd been planning a future with the man who smiled so rarely and had maintained such an icy distance between himself and her since she'd woken in the hospital.

"Maybe I was the only one who wanted progeny. Maybe all he ever wanted was to get his garage rebuilt then get out of our marriage," she reasoned, searching for an answer.

She turned to go into the house. Sarah was still sleeping and, feeling tired herself, Eloise knew she should follow her aunt's example. But she was too restless to lie down. A warm breeze stirred her hair and the soft fragrances of summer teased her senses. Changing direction, she wandered off the porch.

A path leading around to the back of the house seemed to beckon her. Following it, she found herself at the door of a single-story building about the size of a two-car garage. She tried the door and discovered it was unlocked. Going inside, she found herself in what looked like a mechanic's shop. A long workbench ran nearly the entire length of one wall and tools of all sorts were neatly arranged on shelves and in racks above it. More tools hung on the other two walls. Larger power tools that required their own stands were lined up along the back wall.

There was something very comforting about this place, she thought. It had to have been her father's workshop. And from the lack of dust, she was also fairly certain someone was still using it. Jonah, she decided.

"There you are!"

Eloise swung around at the sound of the harried female voice. Sarah was standing in the doorway looking both relieved and perturbed at the same time.

"When I woke and couldn't find either you or Jonah, I called his garage to see if you'd gone into town with him," Sarah continued, regarding Eloise sternly. "He said you'd stayed here so I thought I'd better take a look out here before I panicked and let myself start thinking you'd wandered off and gotten lost."

"I was restless," Eloise explained. "I'm sorry if I frightened you."

"Well, you just come on in the house now and have some iced tea or lemonade," Sarah ordered, holding the door open and ushering Eloise out with a wave of her arm. "We don't want you getting dehydrated."

"I am thirsty," Eloise admitted contritely, wiping a trickle of sweat from her brow.

As the women rounded the house, they heard a vehicle coming up the driveway at a fast clip. An old blue pickup came to a brake-screeching stop a few feet in front of them and Jonah climbed out, slamming the door shut behind him. "I thought you were going to stay inside and rest," he growled at Eloise.

His anger was the most obvious. But she noticed that his hands and arms were streaked with grease, an indication he'd left his garage in a rush, not taking time to even wash up. And behind his fury, she saw worry in the dark depths of his eyes. A warm knot of pleasure curled deep within her. "I've been cooped up inside for weeks now. I needed to get out and breathe some fresh air," she said apologetically, shaken by how much his concern for her pleased her.

His scowl deepened. "Have you had enough fresh air?"

"For now," she replied, finding herself actually searching for more signs of his concern.

His gaze bored into her. "I want your word you won't go out alone, at least for the next few days. There's a lot of land here. You could get lost. And there's rattlesnakes and copperheads."

"I did remember to watch where I walked," she said, immensely enjoying his protective manner. "I'm not sure I knew why but I did know I should."

"I want your word," he repeated curtly.

"I won't go wandering," she promised, suddenly wishing he would take her in his arms.

"Good," he said sternly. Impatience flickered in his eyes. "Now I've got to get back to work."

Eloise stood mutely as he stalked back to his truck. A feeling of abandonment swept through her. My emotions are in a total muddle, she wailed silently, stunned by how important his concern had been to her.

"That man looked downright panicked when he first arrived," Sarah remarked thoughtfully, as the truck sped away.

"Yes, he did," Eloise replied, her conscience suggesting she should experience at least a twinge of guilt for having worried him so badly. Instead her aunt's words brought a renewed feeling of delight.

"Now let's get you inside and get some liquid down you," Sarah ordered, again becoming the commanding mother hen.

As Jonah's truck disappeared around a bend, Eloise nodded and accompanied her aunt inside.

"And I'll warn you now, dinner tonight is going to be bland," Sarah said, leading the way to the kitchen. "Dr. Green called to tell me he'd forgotten to instruct me to keep your food simple."

Eloise was sure Jonah was behind this. She'd thank him when she got the chance. A small thrill of excitement raced through her at the knowledge that she had a good excuse to seek him out alone.

The sudden thought that he was her husband and she shouldn't need an excuse to seek him out alone abruptly dampened the thrill. Forcing herself to face the facts, she reminded herself he'd made it abundantly clear he had no interest in her company. She called herself a fool for wanting him to take her in his arms and, especially, for feeling abandoned when he left.

But even while her pride demanded that she avoid him, she found herself arguing that he had come running when he thought something might have happened to her. Exhaustion threatened to overwhelm her as she sat down at the kitchen table and began to sip the lemonade. "I think it's time for me to take a nap," she announced, forcing herself to her feet.

"That doesn't surprise me," Sarah responded. She gave Eloise a motherly smile. "You don't want to go getting bags under your eyes. You want to look your best for that handsome husband."

Yes, she did, Eloise confessed to herself as she went upstairs. In the next instant she was again berating herself for acting the fool. He'd made it clear he wanted free of their marriage. Had she no pride? she demanded.

But even as this question resounded through her mind, she was again recalling the worry she'd seen behind his anger. A low growl of frustration escaped. What had their marriage been like? Why did she feel so drawn to a man who was so determined to keep a distance between them?

"I refuse to believe I was so weak-minded, I could care for a man who cared nothing for me," she seethed under her breath.

Lying down on the big bed, she stared up at the ceiling. A loneliness so intense she felt hollow inside encompassed her. The image of Jonah lying beside her suddenly filled her mind and the loneliness faded. I think I should learn a little more about my husband and our marriage before I set his suitcases on the front porch, she decided.

The thought that she could be courting disaster taunted her. Intuitively, she knew this was a strong possibility. Still, Jonah's image remained strong as she drifted off to sleep.

A faint whiff of garlic and onions greeted Eloise as Sarah woke her with the news that dinner would be ready soon. Obviously even a doctor's orders couldn't totally control her aunt's creativity in the kitchen, she mused a little later as she made her way downstairs to discover the smell permeating the lower floor of the house.

She was helping Sarah by taking the corn bread out of the oven when Jonah entered.

"I was under the impression Eloise was supposed to be on a *bland* diet," he said reprovingly.

Sarah turned to him with an "I knew it" scowl. "Is there an honest medical reason for that or did you and the doctor cook that one up to suit *your* taste?"

"I simply called Doc Green to make certain we'd gotten all our instructions right," he returned, regarding Sarah with a steady commanding gaze.

He would have intimidated most people with that look, Eloise thought but her aunt merely cast him a haughty glance. "There is nothing more boring than bland pot roast. Besides, garlic and onions are good for the blood. That's common knowledge. And Eloise looks as if she can use some strengthening up."

Eloise had ordered herself to keep her emotions under tight control where Jonah Tavish was concerned. But in spite of her self-cautioning, his attempt to look after her welfare brought a glow of pleasure. Then he turned his attention to her.

His gaze was cool and impersonal. "She does look pale," he conceded.

Eloise scowled, the warmth she'd been experiencing vanished. She'd taken the time to put on a light coating of makeup and fix her hair into a style she thought looked at least a little appealing but he was making her feel like something that had been dragged in out of the rain. "If you two are finished discussing my care and feeding, I'd like to eat," she said stiffly.

Jonah moved to her chair and pulled it out for her. Silently he seated her then started around the table to seat Sarah.

"I can pull my chair out myself," she said, shooing him back with a wave of her hand. "You sit and try some of that dinner before you pass judgment on it."

With a disgruntled, dubious expression on his face, he sat down and forked a small portion onto his plate.

"Well?" she demanded as he swallowed his first bite.

"It's not bad," he confessed and put more on his plate.

Sarah gave a triumphant snort, then applied herself to eating also.

As she began to eat, Eloise covertly glanced at her insular husband. I can't believe I feel so drawn to him, she groaned silently. He's a cold, insensitive clod. However, he was her husband and she had promised herself she'd make some attempt to get to know him better, she reminded herself. "How did your work go today?" she asked.

"Fine," he replied, not even looking at her but continuing to concentrate on his food.

Eloise frowned. Clearly he considered conversing an annoyance. He's an annoyance, she grumbled, feeling like an idiot for finding any pleasure in a few exceedingly brief shows of concern from him. "Good," she replied stiffly, and turned her full attention to her aunt. "You've never told me about your trip to Australia."

"It was a delight," Sarah beamed. "I'd always wanted to see the outback, then Beverly Martin called. She's a cousin on your grandmother's side. It seems her daughter, Margaret, was pregnant and having some trouble and Beverly was going to go help but then her husband had a heart attack so she asked me to go instead. It was quite an adventure. I'm happy to report that both Margaret and her baby came through the delivery just fine. Afterward I stayed on to see a bit of the country."

As Sarah continued to describe her trip, between bites, Eloise couldn't stop herself from again glancing at Jonah. He seemed to have completely forgotten the women. He'd picked up the newspaper and was reading it as he ate.

I shouldn't even waste my time thinking about him, she told herself. Then her gaze fell on his hands. She recalled their strength. The instant of unmasked desire she'd seen in his eyes when she'd entered her bedroom after her shower played through her mind and a tremble shook her. A frustration so strong she had to fight back the urge to scream swept through her.

"Just as soon as I've cleared up the dishes, I'm going to bed," Sarah announced, abruptly ending a recounting of a camping trip into the outback.

It was obvious to Eloise that her aunt had noticed her preoccupation and decided it was time to make a discreet exit and allow Eloise and Jonah time alone.

"I'm pretty beat myself," he said, setting aside the paper and forking his final bite of cherry pie into his mouth. "Think I'll go to bed and read for a while."

The sharp sting of rejection pierced Eloise but pride refused to allow it to remain. She didn't want to spend time alone with him anyway, she told herself, wondering why in the world she'd ever married such a man. "I think I'll watch some television," she tossed in nonchalantly.

As they all rose from the table, she insisted on helping Sarah clear the dishes. Jonah helped, too, and Eloise noticed that he steered a path well away from her at all times.

Fool! she chided herself, recalling how she'd drifted to sleep with thoughts of him lying beside her. The only way he was even going to allow her to get within two feet of him was if she roped and hog-tied him. And he couldn't possibly be worth that much trouble, she assured herself.

Chapter Four

Eloise sat in the porch swing and stared up at the night sky. A full moon cast a silvery glow over the landscape. She blinked as the porch light was suddenly flicked on. "I thought you'd gone to bed," she said with an edge of disgruntlement as Jonah stepped out to join her. She'd been trying to relax and he was the last person she wanted to encounter.

"Thought I'd better check on you," he replied.

His patronizing manner irked her. "I'm curious about something," she said dryly.

He cocked an eyebrow questioningly.

"How in the world did you convince me to marry you?"

Leaning a shoulder against the wall of the house, he regarded her with equal dryness. "I didn't. You proposed to me."

She stared at him as a flush of embarrassment traveled up her neck. "I proposed to you?"

His shoulders squared with defiant pride. "Yes."

Well, she had managed to land in the hospital by trying a stupid stunt in front of group of onlookers, she reminded herself. Still, she refused to believe she hadn't exercised some restraint in her life. After all, hadn't everyone been telling her how conservative she normally was? "If you try to tell me I got down on my knees and begged, I'll call you a liar."

The hint of a grin played at one corner of his mouth. "It was more like a business proposal."

That, at least, sounded more reasonable if anything about their marriage could be considered reasonable, she thought. She studied him narrowly. "What kind of business proposal?"

"You said you wanted a husband."

"I just barged into your home one day and said I wanted a husband?" she choked out, her embarrassment multiplying.

"It kind of surprised me, too," he admitted.

She searched his face for any hint he might not be telling her the whole truth. "Did I say why I wanted a husband or why I chose to ask you?"

"You said you'd always planned to be married before you were thirty. You also said you were sick and tired of playing the dating game. You were never sure whether the man you were seeing was really interested in you or your money."

"I just stood there and told you that," she demanded, finding this very difficult to swallow.

He shifted uneasily. "You'd been seeing Mark Thompson. He's Paul's son. The two of you'd broken up a few weeks earlier. I guessed you'd discovered he was more interested in your money than in you."

"So I was on the rebound." Eloise drew a mental sigh of relief. At least she had a reason for behaving so outrageously. Granted it was a foolish reason, but it was a reason.

His expression darkened. "I've never taken advantage of a woman. I told you I thought you were on the rebound and should take some time to think before you did something you would regret."

She regarded him cynically, her expression letting him know she didn't totally believe his claim of fair play. "Apparently I didn't take your advice."

He met her skepticism with cool dignity. "You told me you couldn't be on the rebound because you never had any deep feelings for Thompson. You said you'd tried to convince yourself you did but you couldn't. Then you'd discovered he was only courting you because he wanted your money so you'd dumped him."

She frowned in continued disbelief. "I did that and then came running to you with a proposal of marriage?"

"You waited a couple of weeks after your split with Thompson. When you came to see me, you looked dressed like a lawyer ready to take on a court battle," he returned.

From somewhere deep within, Eloise knew he was telling the truth. She groaned at the stupidity of her behavior. "Why you?"

Ice entered his eyes. "I might not have been the best choice, but I wasn't the worst choice you could have made."

Her embarrassed flush returned. "I apologize. I didn't mean it that way, exactly," she said, trying to soothe over the insult she'd just thrown at him. "It's just that we're so different."

"That was one of the reasons you came to me," he replied dryly. "You said you were also tired of being asked to family functions and then treated like an unwanted intruder. You figured if you and I were married, your mother could exclude you from her invitation list using me as an excuse. That would give both you and her a socially acceptable means of avoiding each other."

Eloise drew a shaky breath. "It seems I owe you an apology for some very boorish behavior on my part."

He shrugged and his expression became shuttered. "You were being honest. I've never minded people being honest with me. And you made me a fair offer. My garage had burned down and I was having trouble borrowing the money to rebuild. You said you'd give me the money I needed."

She frowned at him in frustration. "But you're paying me back."

His shoulders straightened. "I told you, I don't take advantage of people."

So Mr. Jonah Tavish was both proud and moralistic. But what did that make her? "You're telling me I chose you because I knew you were in financial difficulty and were socially unacceptable to my mother?" she said. A sense of humiliation that she'd felt she had to stoop so low to find a husband spread through her.

"That was part of it."

She caught an underlying edge in his voice and knew he was holding something back. "What was the other part?"

He shifted away from his leaning position against the wall, straightened to his full height and hooked his thumbs into the pockets of his jeans, squaring his shoulders even more. "You knew there was a physical attraction between us. We'd kissed once."

"We'd kissed once?" she repeated questioningly, the vague memories of being in his arms coming back to taunt her.

"It'd happened a couple of months earlier," he elaborated. "For the past couple of years, I'd hired your firm to do my taxes. You'd come by one evening to go over some figures. I'm not real sure just how it happened exactly. You smelled real good. It was some sort of soft perfume you were wearing. And I found myself noticing the cute way you chewed on your pencil."

A growing huskiness in his voice was causing heat to spread through her. Her tongue came out to wet suddenly dry lips.

He frowned self-consciously. "I guess I was feeling particularly lonely that night."

"Gee, thanks," she shot back. The warmth turning to a chill.

He scowled impatiently. "I knew the two of us didn't belong together."

"But you kissed me anyway," she prompted, needing to know what had happened that night that had caused her to choose him to propose marriage to.

His frown deepened. "It was a mutual thing. You got finished and got up from the chair you'd been sitting in. Then you stretched as if your back had gotten stiff. You've got one hell of a good figure and I couldn't help noticing. When you looked at me, you saw me looking at you. I figured you'd give me a get-lost glance and hightail it out of there. Instead I saw you looking at me with a glimmer of interest.''

He drew a terse breath. ''I couldn't resist touching your cheek. I figured you'd slap me. But those gray eyes of yours seemed to grow darker and you took a step toward me.''

Eloise's legs felt weak and she was glad she was sitting. If she'd been standing, she was sure she would have been moving toward him now just as he described her moving toward him then.

''The next thing we knew, we were kissing,'' he continued gruffly. ''Guess I tasted as good to you as you did to me because that was one heck of a kiss.'' A coldness entered his voice. ''But it ended there. You suddenly pushed away from me and I could see you were shocked by your behavior. We both agreed the kiss shouldn't have happened, that it was merely due to a momentary lapse of sanity. And we agreed to forget it.''

Obviously she hadn't, Eloise mused. She'd come back and asked him to marry her. ''And did you forget it?'' she heard herself asking.

''It's a little hard to completely forget something like that,'' he replied levelly.

''So we got married because I wanted a husband, you needed money and we had a strong physical attraction for each other,'' she said, summing up the basics of what he'd just told her.

He nodded. ''That's about it.''

She recalled Charles telling her that she'd been considering having children. She wondered how Jonah had felt about that. "And how was our marriage working out?" she asked.

"Obviously not so good or you wouldn't be having so much trouble remembering. But then I've never had any romantic illusions about marriage," he returned dryly. Abruptly he stalked inside, leaving her alone on the porch.

It was clear to her now that her amnesia had convinced him she was unhappy with their arrangement. That would explain his coolness toward her. The urge to go after him was strong. But what would she tell him? The truth was that her amnesia could be emotional and might be caused because she wanted out of this marriage. Maybe after she'd talked to Charles, something had happened to cause her to have second thoughts.

Her head began to throb. Sighing from frustration, she went inside and up to her bed.

Eloise lay staring out at the predawn sky. When she'd come up to bed last night, she'd fallen immediately to sleep. But when she'd woken half an hour ago, saw that it was barely four and tried to go back to sleep, she'd been unsuccessful. Her conversation with Jonah kept playing through her mind.

Giving in to her inability to fall back to sleep, she got up, dressed in a pair of jeans and a cotton shirt and went downstairs. Entering the kitchen, she discovered Sarah seated at the table working the crossword from yesterday's newspaper.

Her aunt, she confessed silently, intimidated her a little. Still any company other than Jonah was preferable to being alone with her thoughts.

Sarah smiled at her in greeting. "I see you're still on hospital time. Hopefully in the next day or two, both of us will get back to a more natural time clock."

Remembering she'd never actually thanked her aunt for flying all the way from Australia to be with her, Eloise said, "I appreciate you coming to stay with me."

"Since I retired from the military, I try to keep my docket open for family," Sarah replied. "'Course, once in a while, when a case interests me, I still do a little private nursing." An adventurous gleam sparked in her eyes. "I've even gone on location to take care of injured movie directors and actors." She gave Eloise a warm smile. "But I'd have come to take care of you no matter what."

For the first time since she'd awaked with amnesia, the feeling of being truly loved enveloped Eloise. Walking over to her staid-featured, brightly-dressed aunt, she gave her a hug. "Thank you," she said, gratefully.

Sarah gave Eloise a hug back then her manner became authoritative. "I know you're a little frightened right now. That's only natural. But you're going to be just fine."

Feeling as if she'd just been given an order, Eloise had to fight down the urge to salute. "Yes, ma'am," she said instead, then continued on her way to the coffeepot.

After pouring herself a cup of the hot brew, Eloise seated herself in the rocking chair by the window. A large basket containing yarn sat next to the chair. Taking a longer look, she saw a small assortment of knitting needles sticking out one side. Shoved in on the other side were a couple of pattern books and a bundle of crochet hooks. A sudden strong sense of familiarity convinced her this basket and its contents were hers.

Reaching down, she lifted one of the skeins to discover a partially completed pair of baby's booties. She wasn't certain why but instinctively she immediately returned the skein so that it again hid the tiny feet warmers.

Groaning mentally at her inability to remember, she sipped her coffee as she rocked slowly.

"You look like a woman with a lot on her mind."

Eloise glanced at her aunt to find Sarah studying her with motherly concern. "I bought myself a husband and now I can't remember if I was pleased with my purchase or not." She frowned at herself. She couldn't believe she'd been so open. But then everyone in town already assumed her money had been the basis of her marriage.

"And how can you be so sure Jonah married you for your money?" Sarah asked.

"I asked him about why we got married and he told me."

Sarah frowned thoughtfully. "Jonah doesn't strike me as the kind of man who could be bought."

"It was more of a mutually beneficial arrangement," Eloise conceded. "He got his business rebuilt and I got a husband." Out of fairness, she added quickly, "However, he is paying me back all the money I gave him to rebuild."

"So what he really got was a loan for marrying you," Sarah clarified.

Eloise nodded. "That wasn't the bargain I offered him but it's what he wanted."

"And you got a husband." Sarah repeated Eloise's words. She studied her niece levelly. "Do you have any idea why you wanted a husband so badly you were willing to cut a deal?"

"Jonah told me that I told him I wanted to be married before I was thirty and didn't have any prospects. He claimed that I was feeling frustrated because I couldn't tell if a man was after me or my money so I decided to take the guesswork out of the equation."

Sarah nodded slowly. "The part about not knowing if a man was after you or your money seems reasonable. That could be very frustrating. And you wanting to be married before you were thirty sounds a lot like you. You've always had a tendency to plan out your life. But I never thought you were quite so rigid." Interest sparkled in Sarah's eyes. "Did he happen to mention why you chose him?"

Eloise grimaced self-consciously. "He said it was because I wanted to give myself and my mother a good excuse to exclude me from her social calendar."

Sarah's gaze narrowed on Eloise. "Now that I won't buy. You've never had any trouble standing up to your mother. Besides, pleading a headache is much easier than buying a husband."

The self-consciousness on Eloise's face increased. "He did mention that we'd kissed once. It seems we had a strong physical attraction."

Sarah grinned broadly. "Now that sounds much more reasonable than anything you've told me so far."

"And I did get the impression that his coolness toward me could be because he thinks I have the amnesia because I want to forget our marriage ever happened," Eloise added.

Sarah nodded sharply. "That seems very probable. I haven't known him long but I do know he's a proud man."

Eloise drew a shaky breath. "The problem is he could be right. I don't know."

"You have gotten yourself in a pickle," Sarah sympathized.

Eloise squeezed her eyes tightly shut. "I wish I could remember," she seethed through clenched teeth, trying to will her memory back.

"You're only going to give yourself a headache," Sarah warned.

Knowing her aunt was right about the headache, Eloise drew a deep breath and opened her eyes. Looking out the window, she saw the sun rising over the horizon. Jonah's grim image suddenly filled her mind and a range of emotions from desire to anger and frustration swept through her, leaving her feeling drained and shaken. "I just hope I remember soon," she murmured under her breath.

"You can catch more bees with honey than with vinegar," Sarah said sharply as she sat Jonah's breakfast in front of him.

"Is that a warning that I'd better eat these pancakes and keep my mouth shut about whatever you put in them?" he replied wryly.

"There's nothing you wouldn't expect in them except for a few blackberries I found out by the fence by the barn," she returned snappishly. Her gaze leveled on him. "I was making an observation regarding behavior in general."

"Maybe Jonah isn't interested in attracting any bees," Eloise interjected. Immediately she wondered what had made her say that. Was her subconscious trying to tell her something?

"I've never enjoyed being stung," he replied, his tone implying she was correct in her assumption.

Sarah shook her head. "Only living thing I've ever known less amicable than you was an old cur dog who'd been badly treated as a pup and refused to let anyone get close for fear they'd hurt him."

"Women," he muttered, determinedly ignoring both Sarah and Eloise as he smeared butter on his pancakes.

Sarah's unexpected analogy had startled Eloise. But what really shook her was the shadow of uneasiness she'd seen cross Jonah's features. Recalling what she knew of his past and the fact that he'd married her because he had no illusions about marriage, it occurred to her that Jonah's coolness toward her might simply be his normal behavior. If so, their marriage must have been an uncompanionable, uncommunicative union, she thought. Except for the time they spent in the bedroom, she amended. As for her wanting children, maybe that was exactly what the situation was...she wanted children. Jonah probably didn't care. But why put him in her will? she wondered. Mentally she groaned. Every time she thought she was beginning to understand, more question marks arose.

Chapter Five

Sarah pulled into the large parking area beside a two-story structure that had obviously once been a private residence. In the midst of a circular flower garden in the center of the front lawn was a wooden sign inscribed with the words: Thompson and Orman Associates, Certified Public Accountants. "Now remember, you're not here to work," she said as Eloise reached for the door handle. "The doctor was very explicit about you taking at least two more weeks to rest and relax."

"I remember," Eloise replied. She'd been too restless to sit around the house all day. When Sarah had announced she needed to go into town to buy groceries, Eloise had insisted on coming along. But instead of continuing to the store, she'd given her aunt money and asked Sarah to drop her off at her office.

They'd had to look the address up but Hornsburg was a small town and Thompson and Orman Associates had not been difficult to find.

"I'll be back as quickly as I can," Sarah said as Eloise climbed out of the car.

"Don't rush," Eloise replied. Then closing the door, she waved goodbye and started up the flower-lined walk.

A faint sense of familiarity teased her but no solid memories came unlocked.

"Mrs. Tavish." Mary Howe rose from her desk, surprise on her face as Eloise entered. The surprise was quickly replaced by a smile. "It's so nice to see you out and about."

Eloise smiled back. "It's nice to be out and about."

"My goodness, is that Eloise I hear?" Paul Thompson's voice boomed from beyond a partially closed office door.

"I thought I'd come by and see if anything sparked a memory," she said as he came striding out and took her hand in his.

"Well, does it?" he asked, his expression immediately becoming fatherly and solicitous.

Eloise let her gaze travel slowly over the reception area. "Not really," she replied with a disappointed sigh.

"Well, you did take a very hard blow to the head," Paul reminded her.

"I knew you should have stayed away from those motorcycles," Mary interjected. "I had a cousin who lost a leg because of one."

"I suppose you're right," Eloise conceded, then was surprised to experience a small surge of rebellion deep within. Apparently a part of her must have enjoyed being on a motorcycle. Probably the same part that convinced me to marry Jonah Tavish, she thought cynically. In the future, it would be advisable to turn a deaf ear to suggestions from this unorthodox portion of her personality, she decided.

Not wanting to discuss her stupidity, Eloise returned her attention to Paul. "I was wondering if I could take a look at my office."

"Of course." With his hand pressed lightly against her back, he guided her down the hall. "But I don't expect you to do any work," he said in a fatherly voice as they walked. "Dr. Green called me and ordered me not to allow you to come back too soon. I've hired Henry Persell part-time and he'll be able to take up the slack until the doctor declares you as fit as a fiddle once again." Coming to a halt in front of a door with her name engraved in a wooden placard screwed onto the door, he opened it and stepped aside for her to enter.

Entering, she let her gaze travel slowly around the interior searching for something that would spark a memory. The room was large. Bookshelves lined three walls. The fourth wall was mostly windows providing an open, sunny atmosphere. At one end of the room was a wide desk with a couple of wooden chairs fronting it. At the other end was a table with several very comfortable chairs surrounding it. She experienced a sense of belonging here but nothing more tangible.

Paul closed the door and stood studying her, the fatherly concern on his face increasing. "Is Jonah treating you all right?" he suddenly asked bluntly.

Eloise was surprised by the worry in his voice. He actually sounded as if he expected Jonah to mistreat her. "He's been the perfect gentleman," she replied.

Embarrassment showed on Paul's face. "I didn't mean to imply he wouldn't be," he said quickly. "It's just that I've never trusted him."

Eloise experienced a wave of irritation. "Jonah might not be the most social person in the world, but he is an honest, decent man," she said, then was shocked by how quickly she'd come to her husband's defense.

"I admit he does seem to be," Paul conceded. "And I know you've always thought I disliked your choice of Jonah Tavish because I wanted you and my son to get married," he continued, his voice becoming even more fatherly. "But the truth is, I've just always thought you could have found someone more suitable."

"Perhaps," Eloise admitted.

Paul smiled with relief as if he felt she was finally getting her senses back.

Again Eloise experienced a twinge of irritation. "I think I'd like to be alone for a little while," she requested.

"Yes, of course." Paul gave her an encouraging smile as he moved to the door. "If you need anything just let me or Mary know."

"Thank you," Eloise said, relief spreading through her as the door closed behind him.

Left on her own, she wandered slowly around the room. Idly she ran her hands lightly over some of the books in the bookshelves. Reaching the table, she found herself smiling at the porcelain figurine of a clown that acted as the centerpiece. She rested her hand on the back of one of the chairs and noted that the soft leather upholstery was soothing to her touch. The room, she admitted, felt comfortable to her. Reaching the desk, she seated herself behind it. This definitely felt like a place where she belonged. She opened the drawers and glanced at the contents. A nervousness that had been building since she'd entered grew stronger.

Rising she walked over to the filing cabinet and pulled out a folder. Then again seating herself at the desk she began leafing through the papers inside. Relief washed over her. She understood the contents and knew what she should do with them.

Frustration swept through her. "I can remember how to do my job, how to eat, how to read, even how to drive a car," she murmured, recalling watching Sarah during the drive into town and knowing she could have been behind the wheel herself. "I just can't remember anything about my personal life."

A knock interrupted her lament. Before she could respond, her door was opened and a strikingly handsome man dressed in a tailored suit entered. He was clean-shaven, with blond hair cut in a conservative style and startling blue eyes. "Dad told me you were here," he said, closing the door then approaching the desk. "It's a relief to see you looking so well."

"Mark?" she guessed, immediately finding herself comparing him to Jonah. He was not quite as tall as her husband but he was better looking in the classic sense, she admitted. Still, she didn't experience even a glimmer of attraction toward him.

Excitement caused the blue of his eyes to seem even bluer. "You remember me?"

Eloise studied him for a moment more, searching for memories. There were none. "No, Jonah told me I'd dated Paul's son. He also mentioned your name."

Mark scowled dryly. "He actually admitted you married him on the rebound?"

Again Eloise felt a prick of irritation. "He said I told him I wasn't on the rebound and he believed me."

"He would have believed anything to get his hands on your money," Mark returned dourly.

Eloise met his gaze levelly. She was in no mood to skirt the truth. "He told me that I had concluded your only interest was in my money."

Approaching the desk, Mark stood looking down at her, a sorrowful expression on his face. "That was a misunderstanding. I loved you. I still love you. I'd like to beat Tavish to a pulp for letting you injure yourself. You could have been killed."

Anger mingled with sincerity in his voice while his eyes traveled over her face like a soft caress. Could she have been wrong about his motives? Eloise wondered. And even if he had been as interested in her money as he was in her, hadn't she married a man she knew was only interested in her money? The thought that she had made a terrible mistake in choosing a husband shook her.

Rounding her desk, Mark cupped her face in his hands. "I know I talked about your money a lot but I'm an investment counselor. Managing money is my job. It's exciting to me. If I was a pilot I'd probably talk about flying all of the time. Men do that. They talk about their careers."

Eloise had to admit he made sense. Sitting motionless, she concentrated on him, trying to feel some bond with this man who looked like the husband she should have chosen. But his touch left her cold. Even those deep blue eyes aroused no warmth within her.

"I know you, maybe better than you know yourself. You've always hated admitting to making a mistake in your personal life. But you made one when you married Tavish. Just let yourself admit it," he coaxed, leaning closer to her. "I'll bet your memory will come rushing back and when it does, you'll know that you and I should be together."

She saw his face moving closer and knew he meant to kiss her. Suddenly Jonah's image flashed through her mind and she jerked free from his touch. "I may have made a mistake but I'm still a married woman and I won't go against my vows. I think you should leave," she ordered stiffly.

For a moment, he hesitated as if considering his options, then slowly he straightened away from her. "You've always been honorable and even though I don't think Tavish deserves your fidelity, I admire you." He traced the line of her jaw. "Just keep in mind, I'll be here if you ever need me."

"Right now, she needs to get home before the ice cream I bought melts."

Eloise swung her attention to the door to discover Aunt Sarah standing there. Turning back to Mark, she saw an impatient glimmer in the blue depths of his eyes, but as he turned to her aunt only a very charming smile showed on his face. "Miss Orman," he said, approaching Sarah and taking her hand in his. "You're looking as lovely as ever."

Sarah flushed with pleasure under his warm gaze. "And you're as much a flatterer as ever," she replied. "But then it never hurts a woman to have something nice said about her. I'm a great believer in enjoying having one's ego stroked occasionally."

Mark's smile grew even warmer and a look of comradeship spread over his face. "I'm glad you've come to look after Eloise. I know you'll see that she remains on the road to recovery."

Eloise thought Sarah was going to begin to glow. "That ice cream is going to melt if we don't get going," she reminded her aunt, rising from the desk and heading to the door.

Mark turned to her as she approached. "Remember you can count on me if you need anything," he said, his voice ringing with sincerity. Turning to Sarah, he added, "You remember that, too."

"How kind," Sarah replied with a smile.

A few minutes later as Sarah guided the car back onto the street, she was still smiling. "That man could charm the fuzz off a peach."

"Do you really like him?" Eloise asked, again wondering if she'd made a terrible mistake by giving him up.

"I enjoy him. He knows how to make a woman feel very feminine and wanted. And I don't think I've seen a better looking man," Sarah replied, then laughed. "But I'm not sure I'd trust him. He's always struck me as being almost too good to be true."

"But if he really was sincere, he would be the perfect husband," Eloise mused.

Sarah cast her a derisive glance. "No one is ever perfect. You simply have to determine which imperfections you prefer to live with and choose your spouse accordingly."

It would seem she'd chosen a man with some major imperfections when it came to the subject of marriage, Eloise thought. In general he was a cynic who didn't believe the institution was viable and in particular he was mostly indifferent toward her. In fact, the only factor she could count in his favor was the way he could cause her blood to heat with the mere sound of his voice. And that is more a dangerous weakness on my part than a point in his favor, she concluded.

Still her curiosity about him remained strong and was growing stronger by the moment. "Would you mind driving by Jonah's gas station? It's supposed to be right on Main Street," she requested. "I'd like to see the place."

Sarah nodded her understanding and turned into a parking lot to make a U-turn. "He gave me explicit instructions on how to get there in case we needed gas or an emergency arose while we were in town."

They were nearly to the outskirts on the far side of town when Sarah turned on her signal and swung into the wide entrance driveway of a gas station. Four sets of gas pumps sat in front of what was obviously a new building. One portion of the structure was a small store of sorts where customers entered to pay for gas. The walls were lined with packaged assorted vehicle parts... belts, spark plugs, etc. The larger portion of the building housed three mechanics' bays. Cars that looked as if they were waiting to be serviced were neatly parked nearby. Clearly the majority of Jonah's business was doing repairs and tune-ups, Eloise realized. Well, Olivia had said he'd learned his trade from the best mechanic in the area, she recalled.

"I might as well fill up the gas tank while we're here," Sarah said, pulling up to one of the pumps.

"Sure," Eloise replied absently, continuing to survey the establishment.

"Mrs. Tavish." A dark haired teenager grinned broadly with recognition as he came out of one of the bays and jogged to the car. "It's really great to see you out of the hospital. You gave us quite a scare. Ain't never seen Jonah look frightened before but he turned near paper white when you took that spill."

Again Eloise recalled the concern she'd seen on her husband's face when she'd first woken in the hospital. The thought that maybe he wasn't as indifferent to her as he seemed to be crossed her mind. A spark of what felt like pleasure flared deep within her. And I'm probably the biggest fool in the world for caring even the tiniest bit what he thinks, she cautioned herself. She smiled back at the lean boy with grease smears on his cheek and forehead. "It's nice to meet you, Dan," she said, reading his name on his shirt.

The teenager's smile vanished. "I'm Tommy... Tommy Dunn. I just inherited Dan's shirt because we were the same size and I ain't taken the time to take his name off it." Worry etched itself into the young face. "I heard you was having trouble remembering things."

"It's just a temporary condition," Sarah said sharply, as she pulled the nozzle of the pump out of the gas tank.

"Yeah, sure," Tommy replied, giving Eloise a reassuring smile. Apology spread over his face. "Jonah's not here. He had to go to Mrs. Lester's place. She called and said she couldn't get her car started." His grin returned. "She's probably just flooded the engine again but she gets real upset if we try to tell her that instead of going over and checking. Besides, she always brings some homemade cookies the next day. Makes the best peanut butter ones I've ever eaten."

A look of sudden inspiration showed in his eyes. "Hey, how about if I give you a tour of the place. Maybe something will spark a memory."

"I'd like that," Eloise said, already on her way out of the car. Again she told herself she was probably playing the fool to want to learn as much about Jonah as she could. However, he was her husband, at least for the moment, she argued back.

"You two run along. I'll move the car over to the side and wait," Sarah called out to Eloise's departing back.

Absently Eloise gave her aunt a wave as she followed the boy into the small store. Everything was neat and clean.

"We keep a pretty good supply of parts." Tommy motioned toward the shelves along the walls. "Jonah's main business is fixing cars," he continued, confirming Eloise's assessment. A look of admiration came over the boy's face. "He's probably the best mechanic in a hundred miles. Maybe more."

Eloise was surprised by the boy's enthusiastic championing of Jonah. She'd been under the impression her husband did not encourage friendships.

"The bays are over here." Tommy motioned for her to follow him through a door to her right. "When Jonah rebuilt he had three put in," he said as they stepped out into the garage portion of the building. He looked at her anxiously. "You really don't remember any of this?"

"None of it," she replied.

"Like that woman you're with said, you'll remember soon," he declared firmly.

Eloise hoped he was right. Trying to sort out her life seemed to be becoming more and more difficult with each passing day. "The woman is my aunt Sarah," she said as he led her out of the bays and around to the back of the garage.

"Oh, yeah. Jonah mentioned something about your aunt coming to stay awhile." He waved an arm as they rounded the building. "Here's our used vehicle lot." He grinned. "We have to call it that because of the assortment."

They did have an assortment, Eloise noted, from motorcycles to trucks and a couple of ancient-looking cars. An extension of the main building that wasn't visible from the front caught her attention. "I didn't realize the store went back so far."

Tommy looked in the direction of her gaze. "It doesn't. That's a one-bedroom apartment. Jonah's letting me live there rent free while I save money for college. My old man drinks some and he's not great to be around even when he's sober." The boy's smile had vanished and his jaw had tensed. "Jonah don't allow him to come near here." Tommy's shoulders squared with pride. "But I ain't taking charity. I keep an eye on the place, sort of like a night watchman."

Eloise had noticed the boy's limp. Now she wondered if his father had something to do with it. "I'm sure it's a relief to Jonah and me to have you here."

The boy's grin returned. "You've both been real good to me. I appreciate it."

Eloise returned the boy's smile but deep inside she felt a chill. Jonah had said neither he nor she had honestly expected the marriage to last. She was sure he'd built that apartment for himself to use one day.

Her gaze shifted back to the assortment of vehicles. A trim black cycle with red detailing caught her attention. The back bumper was badly dented, there were long scrapes in the paint and the back tire was flat. But in spite of its marred appearance, she was drawn toward it like a magnet.

"Jonah said to put it up for sale," Tommy said, following her.

"It's my bike," she murmured, running her hand over the seat.

Tommy's eyes rounded. "You remember it?"

Eloise was as stunned as he was by her words of recognition. No real memories of her and the bike came into her mind. The realization that it was hers had come strictly from a subconscious level. "No, not really," she replied. "It just felt very, very familiar." Abruptly she turned to the boy. "I want it."

"Sure." Immediately he removed the For Sale sign.

"Would you ask Jonah to bring it out to the farm?" she requested.

"Yes, ma'am." His look of concern returned. "But you will be more careful, won't you? You scared me pretty bad, too."

"I promise," she replied, experiencing an unexpectedly large amount of pleasure from the boy's declaration that he'd been scared, too. For some reason, Tommy must have been particularly important to her, she realized.

He nodded and smiled, then wiped a bead of sweat from his forehead on the arm of his shirt. "We better be getting back to your aunt. The day's getting real hot and you probably shouldn't be out in this sun too long."

Rounding the building, they found Sarah standing in the shade of an old elm tree waiting for them. "Did you have a breakthrough?" she asked hopefully.

"No, not really," Eloise replied.

"She did recognize her bike," Tommy offered encouragingly.

Sarah frowned thoughtfully. "I'd have thought that motorcycle would have been the last thing you'd remember."

"I didn't exactly remember it," Eloise elaborated. "I just sensed a familiarity about it."

Sarah continued to regard her thoughtfully. "An aversion to it would have been a more normal reaction." Her manner suddenly became businesslike and she glanced toward the car sitting in the sun. "I hope you like chocolate marshmallow swirl," she said to Tommy over her shoulder as she began striding to the vehicle.

"The ice cream," Eloise blurted, quickly following after her aunt. "I'm sorry."

Sarah pulled the ice cream carton from one of the brown bags. "This boy looks as if he'd enjoy it more than us anyway," she said, handing the fast softening package to Tommy.

"It's one of my favorites," he declared with a grin.

A few minutes later as they drove out of town, Sarah glanced at her niece. "So the bike felt familiar?"

"Yes," Eloise replied.

"I hope you're not thinking of recreating the event that lost you your memory," Sarah said sternly. "I know a lot of people like to retrace their steps to find things they've lost but in this case, I don't think that's an advisable avenue."

Eloise grinned dryly. "No, I'm not planning to recreate the accident or even a near facsimile."

"I'm relieved to hear that," Sarah replied.

As a comfortable silence descended between them, Eloise sat staring out the front window. She honestly didn't understand why she'd said she wanted the bike. She had no idea what she was going to do with it. Keeping it was about as much of a waste of her energy as continuing to be interested in Jonah, she told herself. Forgetting about both of them would be the smart thing to do. When she got home she'd call Tommy and tell him to put the For Sale sign back on the bike.

But when they did get home, she didn't call the boy. Instead she found herself arguing that the bike had produced a sense of familiarity. Maybe having it around would spark a memory.

Eloise stood staring at the boxes filled with motorcycle parts in the back of Jonah's truck. A dented, badly scraped black fender with red detailing was sticking out of the top of one. "That's not exactly how

I remember seeing my bike earlier today," she said dryly, finally breaking her silence.

"It's taken Tommy a long time to relax and begin to trust people," he replied, standing in the bed of the truck looking dourly down at her. "He's grown real fond of you. After you left he got to worrying you might hurt yourself again. I promised him I'd see that you didn't."

Now she understood why she'd had such a strong reaction to Tommy's concern and it occurred to her that she must have liked the boy very much. Still, she couldn't believe Jonah would go to such lengths. "So you disassembled my bike?" she demanded.

"I figured putting a working bike back into your hands might be like giving a loaded pistol to a child," he replied, jumping down from the bed of the truck. Facing her, he squared his shoulders and met her gaze levelly. "I'll take it to the dump on my way to the garage tomorrow."

The comparison of herself to a child raised her ire. "You will do no such thing," she snapped. "I still want it."

For a moment he looked as if he was going to argue, then he shrugged. "It's your choice."

Watching him unload the boxes onto the driveway, she wondered if she was losing her sanity as well as her memory. She hadn't even known what she was going to do with an assembled motorcycle. What in the world was she going to do with a disassembled one?

Her attention shifted to Jonah. It seemed she'd been making some very peculiar choices for the past year or so, she mused. Going inside, she nearly bumped into Sarah in the hall.

"I was just coming to tell you and Jonah that dinner is ready," her aunt said, then her gaze narrowed on Eloise. "What's wrong?"

Eloise nodded toward the front door. "Jonah brought my bike home...in boxes."

Sarah strode to the door and looked out to see Jonah lifting the last box down from the truck.

"He wanted to take it to the dump but I told him I wanted to keep it," Eloise continued, "but I'm at a loss as to know why in the world I'd want to keep it in that condition. I didn't even know why I wanted to keep it when it still looked like a real bike."

Sarah gave her niece a hug. "You've always had good instincts. I'd suggest you go with them. If they told you to keep the bike then there must be a reason."

Eloise wasn't so sure her aunt was right about her instincts. It could be she was just angry with Jonah and behaving irrationally, but she also wasn't ready to tell Jonah she'd changed her mind. She'd keep the parts around for a few days and then take them to the dump herself.

Chapter Six

Eloise woke in a state of panic. She sat upright in bed, fear pervading her. A rumble of thunder so loud it seemed to shake the house filled the night air. Her gaze jerking to the window, she saw a long thin spear of lightning flash toward the ground. Her fingers entwined in the sheet as her hands balled into fists.

"It's just a storm," she murmured aloud but her words didn't soothe her.

Heavy drops of rain pelted the window. She drew her knees up until she was sitting in a hunched-over ball. "It's just a storm," she repeated but even the sound of her own voice carried no reassurance.

As a second rumble of thunder grew louder, building to a crescendo, abruptly her door was opened. The light in the hall silhouetted a man's form. Then a bright flash of lightning illuminated the intruder and she saw it was Jonah. His hair was rumpled and his only clothing was a pair of jeans. Considering how steadfastly he'd ignored her all evening, she was startled he was there.

"Are you all right?" he demanded gruffly above the sound of the storm.

"Yes," pride forced her to respond.

For a long moment he continued to stand silently, a dark shadow blocking her doorway. A third peal of thunder shook the house and the hall light blinked then went out.

A light suddenly appeared near his hand and she realized he'd taken the precaution of bringing a flashlight. Entering her room, he lit the oil lamp on her dresser. "I'd better check on Sarah. Then I'll be back," he said, barely glancing at her before heading for the door.

The impatient edge in his voice and the fact that he'd avoided looking at her was evidence of his discomfort at being in her room. Pride ordered her to tell him she didn't need him to come back, but fear blocked her throat.

His footfalls could not be heard above the sound of the rain as he made his way down the hall. She suddenly felt terrifyingly alone. Panic bubbled so strongly within her she wanted to scream for him to hurry back. It was only a couple of minutes but seemed like a lifetime before his form again stood blocking her doorway.

"Sarah is sleeping soundly," he said. The hint of a grin tilted one corner of his mouth. "Truth is she's snoring so loudly, I doubt she can even hear the storm."

His attempt at levity surprised Eloise. She'd noticed that although he'd been willing to joke with Sarah every once in a while, especially about her aunt's cooking, he'd never joked with her. In spite of the terror she was feeling, one side of her mouth was actually able to curl upward into a lopsided smile.

He grinned back crookedly and her heart skipped a beat. Then the grin vanished and his expression became unreadable. "If you think you'll be all right, I'm going back to bed."

She wanted to beg him to stay but the coolness in his manner gave her the strength to control that urge. She forced her hands to relax their fisted hold on the blankets and faced him with an assurance she didn't feel. "I'll be fine. You really didn't need to get out of bed in the first place just to come in here." Politeness forced her to add, "But thanks for lighting the lamp."

"You're welcome," he replied, backing quickly out of the doorway, pulling the door closed as he went.

Another boom of thunder rocked the house. Her hands balled into even tighter fists. Tears trickled down her cheeks as she again drew herself into the snuggest huddle possible.

She squeezed her eyes shut, hoping to keep herself from noticing the lightning, and pressed her hands against her ears to block out the sound of the thunder. Still her fear grew and nausea made her stomach churn.

Suddenly the bed shifted, then a pair of strong arms were wrapped around her. "You're going to be all right," Jonah's gruff voice sounded near her ear.

She lifted her head slightly to allow her cheek to rest against his shirtless shoulder. His taut muscles felt like hardened steel. Her grip on the sheet slackened and she raised one hand and let it rest against his chest. The coarse dark hairs beneath her palm had an enticingly rough texture. A sense of being protected crept through her. The nausea subsided and the terror dimmed.

"You've got to be the stubbornest woman I've ever known," he growled. "Why didn't you just admit that you're still terrified of thunderstorms?"

His breath against her skin was sending currents of heat racing through her. "You made me feel like a nuisance."

He raked his fingers through her hair, combing it away from her face. "In a way you are a nuisance. You've always been able to disturb my peace of mind," he said huskily.

His touch was like kindling to a fire. The gruff edge in his voice caused a tremor of excitement. "I like the sound of that," she heard herself admitting. Deep inside a tiny voice cautioned her not to behave foolishly but all she could think about was how deliciously enjoyable being in his arms was.

She felt him draw a harsh breath and heard his heart beginning to beat faster. Her own pulse raced in response.

"You," he growled, "are a difficult woman to deal with."

Lifting her head to look at him, she read the heat in his eyes. Caution was forgotten as desire flamed to life within her. "You're not exactly the easiest man to get along with, either," she returned, but couldn't stop herself from smiling as she spoke.

"I've never known a woman who could look as sexy as you in anything from a business suit to an old cotton nightgown to nothing at all," he grumbled agitatedly.

Her desire burned hotter. She ran her hand over his chest and the flames within threatened to consume her. "You do know how to make a woman feel like a woman," she murmured.

He trembled as if losing a battle with himself, then his lips found hers. His kiss was a hungry kiss. A hunger within her matched his and the storm outside was forgotten as she strove to satisfy his demands.

The taste of his mouth, the touch of his hands filled her senses. Her desire for him grew until she worried she might be consumed by the flames. Unbending from her huddled position, she wrapped her arms around his neck, drawing him down with her. Again from somewhere deep inside a little voice warned this might be foolish but she paid it no heed. Every fiber of her being wanted him to be with her... needed him to be with her.

"No," Jonah rasped, the word a low, curt grumble against her lips. "No," he repeated more forcefully as he lifted his head away. Reaching up, he unwound her arms from around his neck. "We both know this is a mistake."

Eloise lay feeling totally shaken as he rose and stood beside the bed. "You're probably right," she admitted, recalling that this physical attraction seemed to be the only thing they had in common. "I suppose I should thank you for showing so much control." But inside she didn't feel like thanking him. Inside she wanted to scream out of sheer frustration. She wanted to pull him back down with her and tell him they could worry tomorrow about this being a mistake.

The heat in his eyes cooled. He nodded toward the chair by the window. "I'll wait out the storm over there," he said, his expression stoic as if he felt he had a duty to perform and he was determined to complete it.

Eloise felt like an absolute fool. "I'm sure I can make it through this alone," she said with dismissal. "There is no reason for you to feel you have to baby-sit me."

He turned back to her. "Your fear might be irrational but it's strong. Your father died on a night like this. You were barely fourteen, alone in this house with him when he had the heart attack. The lights were out and the phone lines were down. You ran miles through the rain and lightning to the Jefferieses' to get help."

A shiver shook her. For a brief instant she saw the tall, lank man crumpled on the living room floor. In the next moment, she saw herself running through the woods fighting the wind and rain. "I remember," she murmured, then the image was gone.

She looked up to see Jonah watching her questioningly. "It was just a flash," she said.

"Guess that's not something I'd want to remember in too much detail, either," he conceded. Continuing to the chair, he seated himself and gazed out at the storm.

Again she felt like a duty and again the desire to order him to leave was strong. But as the words formed, a fresh rumble of thunder followed by a flash of lightning brought her fear back full force upon her.

Determined to maintain at least a small show of decorum, she propped her pillows up behind her and sat leaning against them, refusing to allow herself to go back into her childlike huddle.

Drawing a deep breath in an effort to calm her still-racing pulse, she assured herself she was glad he'd stopped them from giving in to their lust. Both Mark and Jonah believed she'd blocked out the memories of her marriage because she didn't want to admit to having made a very bad error in judgment. And, she conceded, they were probably right. Most likely, after she'd talked to Charles Polanski about having children, something had happened and she'd determined remaining married to Jonah would be a mistake.

But nothing could be worse than the muddle her emotions were in right now, she wailed silently. If her loss of memory was due to a block, somehow she had to break through it. Abruptly a glimmer of hope emerged. Jonah's explanation of her fear of the storm had brought a flash of memory. Maybe something else he could tell her might bring more. "I suppose you've sat with me through storms before?"

There was a dry expression on his face when he turned to her this time. "We didn't exactly sit out the storms."

The implication behind his words rekindled the fire within her. "I'm sure you were very efficient at keeping my attention diverted," she murmured.

"I did my best," he returned, a huskiness creeping into his voice. Abruptly he scowled at himself and returned his attention to the storm.

The thought that she'd like for him to do his best tonight filled her mind. But the impatience she saw etched into his features as he continued to gaze out the window dampened her ardor. She knew without any doubt that he didn't want to be there. Idiot! she screamed at herself. She again considered sending him away but before the words could even form, another clap of thunder unnerved her.

Sleep was the solution, she decided. All she had to do was doze off and when she awoke both he and the storm would be gone. She forced her hands to loosen their hold on her sheet. But as she started to ease herself down into a more comfortable position, a flash of lightning split the air. Her body tensed so violently she was sure she'd pulled a muscle in her back. Giving up the notion of trying to go to sleep, she sat stiffly.

Just ignore him, she ordered herself, but that was easier said than done. She could see his reflection in the mirror in front of her and even though she commanded herself to look away, her eyes refused to obey. Even more discomforting, the silence between them was as unnerving as the storm. Irritated with herself, she gave in and focused her attention on him.

"Does anything frighten you?" she asked tersely.

"You. I thought you were predictable but you proved otherwise." He scowled as if angry with himself for speaking so openly. Tersely he added, "I blame myself for your accident. I should never have encouraged you to learn to ride a motorcycle."

So guilt was the reason he was hanging around until he was certain she was healed. A coldness spread through her. "I don't want you to feel guilty. From everything I've been able to learn about myself, I'd say I chose my own path."

"You are a hardheaded female," he agreed, continuing to gaze out the window.

The way he continued to avoid looking at her let her know he didn't really want to talk. Again she told herself to ignore him. Instead, she heard herself saying, "You've told me you never expected our marriage to last. Was my hardheadedness one of the reasons?"

He shrugged. "Like I said, I've never had any illusions about any relationship lasting forever." The set of his jaw hardened even more. "And I believe I also mentioned that I wasn't the only one who had doubts about a lasting marriage. You were pretty cynical about the institution yourself. I remember you saying you felt a marriage would only last as long as both parties were deriving some sort of benefit from it."

"That's not so cynical if you're willing to count providing each other with a shoulder to lean on as a major benefit," she rebutted.

This time he did look at her. "I learned a long time ago never to count on leaning on anyone. You do that and you're likely to fall flat on your face."

"Maybe you just never leaned on the right people," she tossed back.

His expression hardened. "The problem is knowing who the right people are."

"You must have trusted Clyde."

"We had a long history," he replied, then returned his gaze to the storm, signaling an end to the conversation.

Studying the taut line of his jaw, she found herself wishing he trusted her. Every instinct told her that although he wasn't the easiest person to get to know, and certainly not the most charming, he was dependable . . . the kind of man a woman could lean on with assurance. But they had a short history, one she couldn't even remember.

And maybe my instincts are all wrong, she cautioned herself. Maybe I want to believe the best of him because I did marry him and I don't want to think I would be so stupid as to choose a man simply because of lust.

Exhaustion even the storm couldn't rival swept through her. Leaning back into the pillows, she closed her eyes.

Eloise awoke to sunlight filling her room. Snuggled into her pillows, she remembered the storm. She also realized she'd fallen asleep in the middle of it. Recalling the reason for her exhaustion, she glanced toward where Jonah had been. The lingering grogginess she hadn't quite rid herself of vanished. He was still there, asleep in the chair.

Leaving the bed, she approached him quietly. A nervousness that she might wake him swept through her. Wryly she smiled at herself. It wasn't as if she was broaching a lion's lair, she chided herself. Still, she moved cautiously.

His hair was rumpled and the urge to comb it with her fingers was strong. Then there was the whiskery stubble on his face. She wanted to rub her cheek against it. But mostly she just wanted to be held in his arms and feel the sense of security she'd felt last night. Then she remembered how much he'd hated being there. There was no security for her in a relationship with him, she told herself curtly.

She considered simply taking her clothes, dressing in the bathroom so as not to rouse him and leave him to wake on his own. But he looked uncomfortable and she felt guilty that he'd probably have a stiff neck and sore back.

"Jonah," she said softly.

"Ellie?" He spoke the name with gruff gentleness.

Her stomach knotted. Had that been his pet name for her or was there another woman in his life he'd actually cared for?

He groaned as he straightened, giving support to her worry that he was going to be sore this morning. Then his eyes opened. "Ellie," he repeated, looking up at her, his gaze still groggy.

There was a tenderness in his voice and on his face that tore at her.

Abruptly his expression hardened. His gaze jerked away from her and he raked a hand through his hair, combing it away from his face. "Looks like the storm's past," he said, levering himself out of the chair.

"Jonah?" She spoke his name questioningly, still shaken by the way just hearing him call her Ellie had felt like a caress.

The cool, distant expression she'd grown used to seeing had returned to his face when he looked at her. "I've got to go to work," he said, then headed to the door.

Left alone in the room, she reached out and touched the back of the chair he'd so recently occupied. The heat of his body still lingered on the fabric. In spite of his frosty, quick departure, she could not erase the gentle sound of his voice when he'd first woken. And there was also the realization that he'd had a pet name for her.

Why couldn't she remember! Her head started to pound. There must be something very painful I don't want to face, she admitted and intuitively she knew she was right.

Chapter Seven

"That was one wild storm we had last night," Sarah said when Eloise entered the kitchen a little later. She smiled at her niece. "But you don't look any worse for the wear."

A gleam in her aunt's eyes caused Eloise to suspect that Sarah had not been as sound asleep as Jonah had thought. As proof this was so, Sarah added, "And how is Jonah this morning?"

In answer to this question, the door opened and Jonah strode in. He looked tired and there was a nick on his chin where he'd cut himself shaving. "I'll just take a cup of coffee and get going," he said, brushing past Eloise and getting a mug from the cabinet. "I'm running late."

She noticed he didn't even look in her direction as he poured himself the coffee, then strode out the back door.

"Guess his night didn't go as well as yours," Sarah mused.

"He spent it in a chair," Eloise replied. "I told him I'd be all right, but he insisted on staying in my room."

Sarah was looking out the window, watching him drive away. "He's not as callous as he'd like people to believe."

"But he's building a thicker skin every day," Eloise returned. A sudden sense of déjà vu swept through her as if this was a familiar thought.

Sarah turned to her. "Calluses are not necessarily permanent. With some determined treatment, they can be softened and eventually they will wear down."

Jonah's kiss came back with vivid recollection. It was quickly followed by the memory of his abrupt withdrawal. "But you have to be allowed to administer the treatment."

"Some patients can be more difficult than others but where there's a will, there's a way," Sarah said with assurance.

Unless you're talking about Jonah Tavish, Eloise rebutted silently. Watching her aunt scramble eggs, she made up her own adage . . . a rock wall will only leave you with scraped hands and knees if you try to scale it. On the other hand, depending on what's on the other side, it might be worth a few scratches, she found herself adding. Silently she groaned at her duplicity.

Eloise stared down at the rain soaked boxes of motorcycle parts. After eating breakfast and helping Sarah clean the dishes, she'd felt restless. She'd wandered outside and almost immediately found her way to where Jonah had lined up the boxes by the side of the house. Now as she stared down at the jumble of disassembled components, she wondered why they were claiming her attention. They were nothing more than junk now.

The sound of a vehicle caught her attention. Glancing around the side of the house, she saw a truck making its way up the driveway. However, instead of stopping at the house, it continued on to the stables. Rounding the house to the back, she watched as a man who looked to be in his late thirties or early forties got out. One of the horses gave a whinny of recognition and approached the newcomer.

"That has to be Jed Beeck," Eloise murmured. Deciding that a ride might be just the cure for her growing restlessness, she headed to her room to exchange her sneakers for a pair of boots and to grab a hat from the shelf.

A few minutes later, as she neared the stables, she heard voices from inside.

"You keep these animals in fine shape," Sarah was saying.

"They're good stock," a man's voice replied. "And I owe Mrs. Tavish. Most people in this town think of her as being pretty standoffish and not real interested in other folks' problems. But I'd have lost my farm if it hadn't been for her. When she heard I was having hard times, she came to see me and offered me money. She said she knew her dad had considered my dad a close friend. I told her I wouldn't take charity no matter how well-meaning. So she offered me this job instead. My farm's doing just fine right now, but I figure I'll keep working for her as long as she wants."

"I'm sure it's a relief to her to know she has someone so competent looking after her horses," Sarah
said.

Concern entered the man's voice. "How is she doing? I sure hope she's going to be all right. I talked to
Jonah the day before you all brought her home. He
seemed worried."

Again Eloise experienced a spark of pleasure that
Jonah had shown open concern for her. Even more,
she had to fight back an urge to burst into the barn
and make Jed elaborate on just how Jonah had behaved and exactly what he'd said. "I've got to stop
caring so much about that man," she murmured to
herself. Again a strong feeling of déjà vu filled her and
she was sure she'd said that same thing to herself before.

"My niece is going to be just fine," Sarah's confident tones floated out to her. "And I'd better be getting back to the house to check on that pie I put in the
oven. Just wanted to come out and make your acquaintance, Mr. Beeck."

"It's Jed, ma'am," the man replied.

Not wanting to be caught eavesdropping, Eloise
decided she should let her presence be known. Pre-
tending she'd just arrived, she called out, "Hello,
anyone around?"

Sarah preceded the farmer out of the stable. "Well,
you look like a woman with a purpose," she said,
eyeing her niece dubiously.

"Thought I'd go for a ride," Eloise replied.

Sarah continued to regard her uncertainly. "I
strained a muscle in my back on that camping trip in
Australia. It's healing quite nicely but it's not well

enough for me to go horseback riding just yet." She turned to Jed. "Do you ride?"

Jed shook his head. "No, ma'am, I just take care of them."

Returning her attention to Eloise, Sarah frowned doubtfully. "You'd have to go alone and I'm not certain that's wise."

Eloise swung her gaze to Jed. "Am I a good rider?"

Looking as worried as Sarah, he nodded. "One of the best," he admitted hesitantly.

"Then I'm sure I'll be just fine," she said confidently.

Jed continued to look concerned. "Even good riders take falls," he said.

"I really think we should check with Dr. Green," Sarah protested.

"I'll be fine," Eloise insisted, heading into the stables. Approaching the saddles and bridles, she realized she knew exactly how to use them.

"I can't believe I can remember something so unimportant and not remember my husband or my marriage," she muttered under her breath.

She was pulling a saddle off its rack when Jed and Sarah joined her. Taking the saddle from her, Jed said firmly, "Looks like you're determined so I'll pick the horse and saddle her for you."

"Blue Lady." She blurted out a name that suddenly flashed into her mind.

"Blue Lady," he said with approval. "She's the most ge..."

He stopped in midsentence and Eloise saw both him and Sarah studying her hopefully. "I just recalled the name," she said, realizing they thought her memory might have returned.

"And you'll keep remembering until you remember everything," Sarah avowed.

Jonah's kiss filled Eloise's mind and again frustration swept through her. She wanted to remember everything right now! Feeling as if she would burst if she didn't do something to get her mind off her dilemma, she reached for a bridle. "Let's get that horse ready," she directed, already on her way out of the barn.

A gray mare came walking toward her. "Good girl," she said, patting the animal's muscular neck. Without any doubt she knew this was Blue Lady. The thought that she knew her horse but not her husband tormented her.

Maybe I didn't think of Jonah and me as being a real husband and wife, she reasoned. With each passing moment she was becoming more certain that something had happened between them she didn't want to remember.

"Maybe you should take a few turns around the meadow before you take off into the hills," Jed suggested, finishing cinching the saddle and taking the bridle from Eloise.

Eloise nodded her consent. A couple of minutes later she was swinging up into the saddle. There she felt totally comfortable. As she took a couple of slow turns around the meadow, she was aware of Sarah standing by the fence near Jed, both of them watching her anxiously. She guided Blue Lady over to them. "Apparently riding a horse is like riding a bicycle," she said, hoping to ease their worry. "Once you learn, you never forget."

"Apparently so," Sarah conceded. "However, you still shouldn't be exerting yourself too much." She glanced at her watch. "I'll expect you back in half an hour and don't go where you can't keep sight of the house."

Eloise considered protesting, then stopped herself. Her aunt was only asking her to take a reasonable precaution. Maybe if she'd practiced some caution during the past year she wouldn't be in the situation she was in today. "Half an hour and I'll stay in sight of the house," she promised.

"I'm still not happy about this," Sarah complained. "Perhaps you should simply ride around in the meadow."

"Really, that's..." Eloise began to refuse this further restriction but was interrupted by the sound of a car approaching.

Waving to the trio by the barn, the driver continued past the house, parking a little ways from them. Eloise recognized Mark Thompson. When he climbed out of his car she saw he was carrying two roses, one yellow and one pink.

"For you," he said, handing Sarah the yellow one as he reached the three gathered by the fence. Then turning to Eloise, he smiled warmly and extended the pink one to her. "I came to see for myself how you'd fared the storm. I know how much you hate them."

"I fared just fine," she replied, accepting the flower out of politeness. I should be flattered, she thought looking down at the fragrant bloom. Instead she was merely impatient to get on with her ride. "I appreciate your concern but you needn't have bothered."

"She was well looked after," Sarah assured him, primly.

"I never doubted for a moment she wouldn't be," Mark replied hurriedly, obviously wanting to remain on Sarah's good side. His gaze returned to Eloise, and his voice took on a tender undertone. "But I'm still worried."

Again Eloise told herself she should feel flattered. Instead all she felt was a vague irritation. Nudging her horse away from him and to her aunt, she extended the flower toward Sarah. "Would you mind putting this in some water." Then turning to Mark, she said, "I appreciate your concern. Now if you'll excuse me, I've been given a half hour for a ride and I don't want to waste it."

His gaze traveled to the other three horses grazing lazily in the meadow. Looking back at her, he frowned abruptly. "Surely you aren't going off by yourself?" He turned to Jed and Sarah. "You weren't planning on letting her go alone."

"We..." Jed began, the uneasiness back on his face.

"I didn't give them a choice," Eloise interjected.

Mark suddenly grinned. "That sounds like the Eloise I know." His expression became businesslike. "However, I still don't think it's wise for you to go riding alone and I'm sure Dr. Green would agree. So I'll come with you."

Eloise wasn't certain why but this did not please her. "You're not dressed for riding."

"Jed, saddle Debit for me," Mark ordered, ignoring her protest. As he spoke, he stripped off his suit coat and his tie and unbuttoned the top two buttons of his shirt. Turning back to her, he said, "Now I am."

For a moment, Jed hesitated, then as if convincing himself he had no choice, he said firmly, "Mrs. Tavish should have someone with her." Before the words were totally out, he was heading for the meadow.

Eloise looked to her aunt for support. "I'll be fine on my own."

Apology showed on Sarah's face then her jaw firmed. "It would be best if you didn't ride alone."

Mark smiled up at Eloise. "You might as well give up. Even if you won't let me ride with you, I'll follow you. As long as I can prevent it, I refuse to allow anything bad to happen to you."

He was certainly protective, Eloise thought. Had she misjudged him? Even worse, had she married Jonah in a fit of disillusionment and was the reason she couldn't remember her marriage because deep inside she now knew she should have married Mark? "All right," she agreed. "Since you're being so insistent and everyone else thinks I need a caretaker, you may ride with me."

Mark performed a stiffly formal bow from the waist. "I am honored." Then straightening, he gave her a mischievous wink before returning to his car and tossing his coat and tie inside.

Watching him, Eloise again told herself she should be flattered by his attention. But still the twinge of irritation remained.

"I'll be expecting you two back in half an hour," Sarah said, as Jed came out of the stable leading a brown gelding, saddled and ready to be ridden.

"Half an hour," Mark promised, swinging up into the saddle.

"I really hate the thought that you might ruin your suit," Eloise said apologetically, finding herself hoping he'd suddenly change his mind and let her go for her ride alone.

"At the most it will get dirty and I can have it cleaned," he replied with an easy smile. They were making their way around the stables and to the wooded mountainside beyond. Glancing over his shoulder, he waved to Sarah and Jed then gave his horse a nudge to bring it alongside hers. In a voice that held a strong note of regret, he said, "Besides, it's been a long time since we've ridden together. I've missed that."

Eloise cast him a warning glance. She was having enough trouble getting her emotions in order. She didn't need or want him putting any pressure on her.

"I'm just talking about us as friends," he said quickly, the underlying wistfulness gone from his voice. "I always felt I could talk to you."

The path had narrowed, making riding side by side impossible. Eloise reined in, letting Mark take the lead. Studying his back, she tried to feel some spark of warm emotion. Surely if she'd seriously considered marrying him, she must have felt some physical attraction, she reasoned. And he was certainly good-looking. But the only reaction she could muster was impatience. "Did I talk openly to you?" she asked, startling herself by the question.

Turning in the saddle, he met her gaze squarely. "Yes."

Eloise had the distinct impression there was something he wanted to say, but instead he turned forward. She did notice that his back seemed more rigid.

Ahead of them the path branched. "Left or right?" he asked.

The urge to go right was strong but something held her back and the word "left" issued from her.

Mark frowned musingly. "During all the times we've ridden on your land, I've never been up the path to the right. Why don't we try that for a change?"

Rebellion bubbled within her. For some reason, she didn't want him taking that trail. "My intuition tells me to follow the trail to the left," she said firmly.

For a moment Mark hesitated, then shrugged. "I've learned it's never wise to argue with a woman's intuition," he said and gave his horse a nudge, guiding it onto the path to the left. They'd gone only a short distance when the path broadened again. Unexpectedly Mark raised his hand, signaling he wanted her to halt. When she did, he turned his horse so he could face her easily. "Look, I made a mistake that shook your trust in me," he said tersely. "I had an affair with Barbara Howard during the time we were seeing each other. When I realized I had honestly fallen in love with you and wanted to marry you, I broke it off. But Barbara was furious...a woman scorned, I guess you could say. Anyway, she was determined to have her revenge. She called you and told you about her and me, only she made it sound as if I was still seeing her."

So it would seem she had a second reason other than money to have caused her to break with Mark, Eloise mused.

"I refuse to stop hoping you will give me a second chance," he finished.

"As I reminded you before, I'm a married woman," she replied stiffly. Silently she wondered how much longer she would be wed but that thought was none of his business. She didn't want more complications in her life than she already had and telling him about an impending divorce might only encourage his attentions. Glancing at her watch, she added, "We'd better be getting back to the stables. My aunt doesn't like to be disobeyed."

A plea entered his eyes and he took her hands in his. "Please, don't be angry with me. I'm trying to respect your marriage vows but that isn't easy when I care so strongly for you." Then releasing her, he gave his horse a nudge and took a trail branching to his left that sloped downhill.

Riding behind him, Eloise tried to sort out her feelings. Learning of his affair could have been the reason she'd run to Jonah Tavish, she admitted. She searched for a sense of a bond with Mark or even some tenderness. But all his presence evoked was indifference and the wish that he'd leave her alone. Surely if I'd truly cared for him I'd feel something, anger even, but something, she thought, frustration again beginning to build within her.

"Thought I'd just hang around and make sure you got back all right," Jed said when she and Mark returned.

Eloise saw the protective look in his eyes and was sorry she'd worried him. She thanked him warmly as he held her horse while she dismounted. Then pleading exhaustion and a headache, she left the men to tend to the horses and went inside. Glancing back toward the stables through the kitchen window, she was irked to see Mark climbing into his car, leaving Jed to unsaddle Debit as well.

Waiting until his car was well down the drive, she went back to the stables. "I'll brush them," she said, reaching Jed as he removed Debit's saddle.

"They was rode lightly. I was just going to release them into the meadow," he replied. "I'll give them all a brushing when I come tomorrow."

Eloise saw Blue Lady looking longingly toward the meadow.

"Don't you worry none about them, Mrs. Tavish," he continued, giving the horse a loving rub on the neck. "You've built them a right nice home here. They've got the meadow and they can get back into their stalls on their own when night comes. I'll see they've always got food and water and brush them down a bit when it's needed."

He gave her an encouraging smile. "And Jonah had me teach him how to take care of them in case something came up and I couldn't make it here. So there's no reason for you to fret."

The image of Jonah astride the roan stallion currently grazing lazily in the meadow suddenly filled Eloise's mind. "Does my husband ride?" she asked abruptly.

"You was teaching him and he was doing real well," Jed replied. "He don't let it show real open but he likes the horses and he respects them. Animals can sense that. I've seen Blue Lady nuzzle him. She don't do that with just anyone, only people she likes. And Cash Flow—" Jed nodded toward the roan "—he comes running whenever Jonah even gets near the fence.''

"Do you like my husband, Mr. Beech?" Eloise flushed when she realized she'd spoken aloud.

Jed looked surprised and her embarrassment grew.

"I'm sorry, that was unfair of me," she said quickly.

Jed regarded her thoughtfully. "I don't know him well enough to like or dislike him. He don't make friends easy. But he's always treated me fairly and honestly and from what I could tell, he treated you good, too." He glanced down the road. "Mr. Thompson has a right nice way with words, especially around women, but I don't know if I'd trust him."

"I think you're right," she replied, all of her instincts agreeing with this conclusion.

Jed nodded and she noticed a glint of relief in his eyes.

A few minutes later, watching him drive away, Eloise breathed a troubled sigh. The horses liked her husband. Her lawyer appeared to approve of him. Even Aunt Sarah, in spite of having had a couple of run-ins with Jonah, seemed to be encouraging Eloise not to give up on her marriage too quickly. And Jed, while cautious, had only good things to say about him.

"Taking a consensus of how others feel isn't going to help," she admonished herself, still embarrassed that she'd asked the farmer what he thought of her husband.

A whinny sounded nearby. Turning to the fence, she saw Blue Lady standing there watching her. "I'm totally confused and frustrated," she informed the horse. "Have you got any solutions to my dilemma?"

"I think you need a nice little nap before lunch," Sarah's voice sounded from behind her. "Your brain and your body need rest to recover from the trauma. You just give yourself some time and pretty soon you'll be right as rain."

"I am tired," Eloise admitted, hoping her aunt was right and that a little more rest and time would bring back her memory.

Eloise awoke in tears. She'd been dreaming. In her dream, she'd been standing looking down at the boxes of parts that had once been her motorcycle. The sight had caused a sadness that had shaken her to the core.

Sitting up on her bed, she brushed at the streams of tears running down her cheeks. "I cannot believe I'm crying over a busted bike," she murmured.

Now fully awake, she stopped the irrational crying. But she was still feeling shaken as she went into the bathroom and washed her face to get rid of any remaining traces of the salty tears.

"How can I feel so sentimental about that stupid motorcycle? I almost got killed on it," she berated her pale image in the mirror.

Abruptly she recalled the fork in the path during her ride with Mark. The urge to go back and take the branch to her right grew.

Quickly she pulled her boots back on, grabbed her hat from the closet and went down to the kitchen. "I want to pack a small picnic," she informed Sarah. "There's a place I have to go."

"Then we'll pack enough for two," Sarah replied, taking the bread out of the bread box while Eloise pulled meat and cheese out of the refrigerator.

"No." Eloise faced her aunt levelly. "I need to go alone."

Sarah frowned sternly. "And where is this place you feel you have to go alone?"

"It's on the mountain." Eloise turned to look out the kitchen window facing the direction in which she'd ridden that morning. "There's a place there I have to go see."

Sarah's frown disappeared and excitement glistened in her eyes. "You've remembered something?"

Eloise shook her head. "No. It's just an urge I have. But it's too strong to resist."

"I don't like you going alone," Sarah protested, watching Eloise making herself a sandwich.

"I have to," Eloise insisted, dropping the sandwich into a bag then hurrying out the back door before Sarah could continue the argument.

Striding to the fence, she whistled and Blue Lady came. "We're going out again, girl," she informed the horse, feeling as if she was talking to an old, comfortable friend.

As if Blue Lady understood, the horse neighed and shook her head in what looked like a gesture of agreement.

All the time she was saddling the mare, Eloise kept glancing over her shoulder expecting Sarah to enter the stable and attempt to forbid her to go. Her jaw hardened with resolve. Nothing her aunt could say would stop her. She didn't want to quarrel with Sarah, but her mind was set. Why following that path was so important to her, she didn't know. All she knew was that it was drawing her.

To her relief, Sarah didn't come. Mounted on Blue Lady, it took every ounce of her control not to urge the horse into a gallop as they moved toward the woods. She was sure her aunt was watching from the kitchen and didn't want to worry Sarah any more than she already had.

An unexpected tranquillity slowly crept through as she entered the woods and followed the path she'd taken that morning. When she reached the fork and took the right branch, the feeling of entering a sanctuary grew stronger. The path she now followed was a steeper uphill grade than the one she'd left but Blue Lady seemed to know the footing well. They had gone quite a ways when Eloise saw a break in the trees signaling a clearing. Entering it, she discovered a huge rock formation. It seemed to jut out from the side of the mountain. Dismounting, she tethered the mare to a nearby tree and made her way to the rock. Climbing up on it, she looked out at the valley below. The sight was breathtaking. This was the place she had sought. That she knew without a doubt. Seating herself cross-legged on the rock, she nibbled at her lunch, hoping the reason for her coming here would burst forth from the recesses of her mind. But no memories emerged.

"Maybe Aunt Sarah's right. Maybe I just need to rest my mind," she said over her shoulder to her horse.

Again Blue Lady neighed and shook her head as if in agreement.

Eloise grinned at the mare. "It's nice to talk to someone who's so amiable."

Blue Lady snorted in acknowledgment of the compliment, then busied herself nibbling some nearby leaves.

Drawing her knees up under her chin and wrapping her arms around her legs, Eloise sat trying not to think but to merely allow the peaceful beauty of this place to blanket her. But even as the sun spread its warmth through her and a mellowness began to descend over her senses, Jonah's image filled her mind. She saw him standing near the edge of the rock, like an unmovable mountain himself, staring down at the valley below.

"What really happened between us?" she murmured.

A whinny from Blue Lady caused the image to vanish. Looking over her shoulder she realized another horse was approaching. Through the trees she caught a flash of reddish brown. In the next moment, the roan emerged with Jonah astride him.

"Sarah called me," he said stiffly. "I figured you'd come here."

She watched in silence as he dismounted and tethered his mount near hers.

"Do you know why this place is special to me?" she asked as he climbed up on the rock and took the exact stance she'd visualized only moments earlier.

He turned to look at her. "You call this rock your 'thinking space.' You consider it your private sanctuary."

A sudden realization struck her. "You've been here before."

"You showed it to me."

Recalling how strongly she'd rebelled against allowing Mark to come here, she frowned. If she and

Mark had been as close as he'd claimed, why hadn't she ever brought him here?

"When I questioned Sarah about her judgment in allowing you to go riding alone, she said you'd gone out this morning and survived just fine." He scowled reprovingly. "You're still recovering from a serious trauma to your head. I can't believe she allowed you to go roaming freely on this mountain on your own, not once, but twice."

"I wasn't alone the first time," Eloise said, feeling it was only fair for her to come to Sarah's defense.

Jonah raised a questioning eyebrow.

"Mark Thompson came by just as I was getting used to being back on a horse. He insisted on riding with me," she elaborated.

Jonah's expression darkened. "I may not be the right man for you but neither is he."

"I think my instincts are trying to tell me that," she admitted. "When we came to the fork in the path, I wanted to come up here but something inside of me refused to bring him here." To her surprise she was sure she saw a glint of pleasure in the brown depths of his eyes, then it was gone and the icy coolness returned.

"If you're wise, you'll follow those instincts," he advised.

She suddenly wondered what instinct had caused her to bring Jonah here. Maybe that was one I shouldn't have followed, she thought.

He motioned toward the path. "It time for you to be getting back to the house."

Again she found herself rebelling against being ordered around but her retort got no further than her throat. The realization that she didn't want to argue with him stunned her. It was as if she was afraid of causing the barrier between them to grow stronger. It can't be any stronger, she chided herself. Still, she gave a shrug and rose.

Attempting to quell her pride, as she walked to her horse she pointed out to herself that the sun was getting hot and his presence had ruined the tranquillity of the place, anyway.

But as they rode back to the house, his silence grated on her nerves. Again he was making her feel like a nuisance and her temper flared. "I'm sorry Sarah pulled you away from your work unnecessarily," she apologized curtly.

"Until the doctor declares you fully healed, you're my responsibility," he replied. His gaze narrowed on her. "I want your word you won't go off on your own again."

This time her pride refused to be subdued. "I am *not* your responsibility."

His gaze bored into her. "I want your word you won't go off alone again."

The set of his jaw told her that arguing would be a waste of her breath. "You have my word," she promised through clenched teeth.

As they continued the ride in silence, she worked on convincing herself he was an overbearing bore and that all that ever had been between them was lust. That certainly seemed to be the most reasonable explanation of their relationship.

Back at the stables, he insisted on unsaddling the horses.

"I need to give Blue Lady a quick brushing," she said with dismissal when he'd hung the last bridle on its peg. "You can go on back to doing whatever you were doing before Aunt Sarah interrupted you."

"I'll just give Cash Flow a quick brushing, too," he returned, finding a second brush and beginning to work on the roan.

Eloise was certain he didn't want to be there but it was clear he wasn't going to leave until she was back in the house. "Done," she said after only a couple of minutes and sent the mare back into the meadow. Then, without a backward glance at Jonah, she strode to the house.

He entered right behind her. Almost immediately she noticed the bud vase containing the two roses sitting in the center of the kitchen table.

"Nice flowers," he said, the coldness in his voice letting her know he'd guessed whom they were from.

"Mark brought them." She confirmed his suspicion.

He regarded her cynically. "Be careful. The man has a way of undermining even the best instincts and wrapping a woman around his little finger."

"No man will ever wrap me around his little finger," she snapped back.

He'd gone to the sink to wash his hands. Glancing over his shoulder, he suddenly grinned crookedly. "Maybe not."

Eloise felt her heart skip a beat at the sight of that smile. The thought entered her mind that if he tried, Jonah Tavish might be able to wrap her around his little finger. But he would never want to, she re-

minded herself. Besides, she would never want to be
that vulnerable to any man, she admonished herself.

Jonah's grin vanished as quickly as it had appeared. His expression shuttered, he dried his hands,
announced he had a garage full of cars to work on and
left.

"That man cares for you," Sarah declared, standing at the window watching Jonah climb into his
truck. "When I called and told him about you going
riding alone, he was furious."

A glow of joy began to spread through Eloise. Immediately she extinguished it. "It's not *caring*, it's
guilt. He blames himself for my accident and feels re-
sponsible for me now," she said.

Sarah frowned at her. "He must have driven like a
madman to get here as quickly as he did and he didn't
even stop at the house. He went directly to the stables, saddled that horse and took off."

Eloise regarded her aunt dryly. "I would never have
thought of you as having such a strong romantic
streak."

"I like to see people who are in love work out their
problems rather than go their separate ways." Sarah's gaze narrowed on her niece. "Act rashly today
and regret it for the remainder of your years."

Eloise was sure she saw a shadow of sadness in her
aunt's eyes. "You sound as if you are speaking from
experience."

Sarah's back straightened. "It's water under the
bridge," she said. "For you, however, there is still
time to avoid making a mistake."

"The problem is, I'm not sure if the mistake would be to try to make my marriage work or simply allow it to be broken," Eloise confessed.

Sarah gave her niece a hug. "All I'm suggesting is that you give yourself time and don't make any rash decisions."

"The decision might not be mine to make."

Sarah looked her niece in the eye. "You have never been one to shrink from a challenge."

A challenge was a good way to describe Jonah Tavish, Eloise thought. An impossible feat might be a better description, she amended. Suddenly not wanting to think about him any longer, she said, "What's this business about water under the bridge? What happened between you and the man you loved? With your tenacity, I can't believe you just gave up on him."

"Ward Anders and I were both very proud people. Neither of us would bend." Sarah studied her niece closely. "The Eloise I knew was a lot like me. Don't make the same mistake I made."

Again Eloise saw the sadness in her aunt's eyes. Then abruptly Sarah's expression became stern. "And now that we've had this little talk, it's time for me to do some letter writing I've been neglecting and for you to wash up and take a nap. Also there's a list of phone messages for you. Your uncle Prescott called and so did your aunt Maude and aunt Belinda. I told my brother and sisters you'd get back in touch with them when you remembered who they were."

"Thank you," Eloise said, grateful she hadn't had to try to make conversation with people who were, for the moment at least, strangers to her.

"Your cousin Irene also called." A thoughtful expression spread over Sarah's face. "I should go visit her." Then abruptly, her attention returned to Eloise. "But first I need to get you healed. Now, you go on upstairs and take a nap."

Aunt Sarah was full of surprises, Eloise thought as she made her way to her room. She would never have pictured her aunt as a romantic and certainly not as a romantic with a lost love in her past.

"Clearly people are not always as they appear on the surface," she mused a little later as she lay on her bed. A grimness descended over her features. "However, in Jonah's case, it's my guess his surface is much too tough to penetrate. And," she added, "even if I were to succeed, I might be real disappointed by what I find."

Chapter Eight

Wiping grease and dirt from her hands onto a rag, Eloise stood staring down at the pile of motorcycle parts now lying on the floor of the workshop. She'd tried to follow her aunt's order and nap but had been too restless to sleep. After tossing and turning for several minutes, she'd come downstairs, wandered through the house then gone outside. Her path had taken her to the boxes containing her disassembled bike. Not really understanding why, she'd gotten a wheelbarrow and moved the contents of the boxes into the workshop.

"I thought you were going to rest."

Eloise turned to see Sarah standing in the doorway. "I tried but I couldn't."

"You can lead a mule to water but you can't make him drink," Sarah said with resignation.

"I thought it was a horse...you can lead a horse to water," Eloise corrected.

"Mule seemed like a more appropriate analogy," Sarah returned. Then her gaze shifted to the pile of parts on the floor. "What in the world are you going to do with that junk?"

"I'm going to sort it." The words had come out without thought and Eloise was as surprised by her answer as her aunt appeared to be.

"What in the world for?" Sarah demanded.

"I'm not sure," Eloise confessed. "It just sort of seems like the right thing to do."

Sarah looked from her niece to the clutter on the floor and then back to her niece. After a moment she said, "Well, I guess you can't get yourself into any trouble doing that." Smiling encouragingly, she added, "Have fun," then left.

"Sort them? I said I was going to sort them?" Eloise muttered, wondering what insanity had caused her to choose this course of action. "Maybe I should reconsider that decision."

But even as she tried to convince herself this would be a ridiculous waste of her time, she reached down and picked up a spark plug and began wiping it with the rag she'd been using to remove the grease and grime from her hands.

Later, when Sarah returned to the workshop to inform Eloise that it was nearly dinner time, Eloise was shocked by how fast the time had passed.

"Looks like the sorting is going slowly," Sarah remarked, looking from the large pile still in the middle of the floor to the smaller piles along the far wall.

"I'm cleaning each piece as I go," Eloise explained.

Sarah regarded her thoughtfully. "Well, you do seem to know what you're doing. I suppose some of your father's love of tinkering rubbed off on you."

"So it would seem," Eloise replied, realizing she felt almost relaxed for the first time since she'd regained consciousness in the hospital.

But as she washed up for dinner, her tension returned and she knew it was because she would be seeing Jonah. She glared at her image in the bathroom mirror. "You will not let that man's presence bother you," she ordered. "Ignore him!"

Entering the kitchen, her back stiffened as if preparing for battle. Glancing at the table she saw that only two places were set. The thought that Aunt Sarah planned to leave her and Jonah alone shook her.

"Jonah can't make it for dinner," Sarah said, noticing Eloise's line of vision. "He called to say he had to work late and would have Tommy run out and get him something from a fast-food place."

Lucky him, Eloise thought as Sarah sat a casserole on the table.

"It's paella. I learned how to make it when I was working for a movie director who was filming in Spain. It's the Spanish version of my grandmother's getting-rid-of-the-leftovers soup. But instead of a stock base, you use rice and toss in whatever you have lying around in the refrigerator that suits your taste." Sarah frowned at the worried look on Eloise's face. "Try it before you turn your nose up at it."

Obediently Eloise dished some onto her plate, then forked a bite into her mouth. The strength of the spices threatened to make her nose run. "It's definitely tasty," she replied diplomatically.

Sarah nodded approvingly. As she began to eat, a gleam of amusement sparkled in her eyes. "Actually I was hired by the studio to care for the director. He had a broken leg and a broken nose from a skiing accident. The break in the leg was bad enough to confine him to a wheelchair. But he didn't believe in letting that stop him from going barhopping at night. Of course I had to go with him."

As Sarah launched into a description of the director's antics, Eloise realized the woman had led a rather adventurous life. But as entertaining as Sarah's stories were, they did not hold Eloise's attention. Instead she found herself glancing toward Jonah's empty chair.

"You miss him," Sarah said abruptly.

Eloise turned to her aunt to see Sarah nodding at Jonah's chair.

"Don't be ridiculous," Eloise replied.

Sarah raised a skeptical eyebrow.

Eloise drew a terse breath. "All right, I do miss him," she admitted grudgingly. "I don't know why I should. Even if he was here, he'd just sit there not saying anything."

A wistful look came over Sarah's face. "I used to just like being in the same room with Ward. We didn't have to say anything or even be sitting close. I simply loved being able to look over and see him."

Eloise frowned. "I find it difficult to believe I could feel that way about Jonah. He certainly doesn't feel that way about me."

"Before you make any decisions, maybe you should put a little more effort into getting to know him," Sarah suggested.

Eloise's frown deepened. "I have tried. But he's got a barrier around himself as thick as any wall ever built."

"It only takes a small crack to make a wall begin to crumble," Sarah declared.

Eloise found it difficult to picture Jonah's wall cracking much less crumbling.

As they washed dishes, her restlessness returned full force. "I'm going to go back and sort some more," she informed her aunt when they finished.

Sarah frowned reprovingly. "You shouldn't overdo it," she cautioned again.

"I'm using the same amount of energy as I would sitting in a chair knitting," she argued. "Besides, it relaxes me."

Reluctantly Sarah yielded. "In that case, go ahead. But I expect you to use some common sense and quit when you're tired." Promising she would, Eloise found some clean rags then went back to the workshop. Seating herself cross-legged on the floor, she picked up the fender. As she began to wipe it clean, an image suddenly flashed into her mind. It was Jonah and herself, both on their knees beside a partially built bike. He was showing her how to attach the carburetor. His expression was intense as if he was relating something he felt was important, still she had the feeling he was enjoying playing the role of teacher.

She sat motionless, frozen by shock. She'd assumed her father had been the one to teach her mechanics. Now she realized it had been Jonah. So they had done more together than simply share a bed.

Hoping she would remember more, she began to work once again.

"Do you realize how late it is? You're supposed to be getting your rest," a gruff male voice broke into Eloise's concentration.

She looked up to see Jonah standing in the doorway of the workshop. He looked tired and irritated.

Glancing at the clock on the wall, she saw that it was nearly midnight. "I've been so busy, I didn't notice," she replied calmly, refusing to allow him to rattle her.

He continued to scowl down at her. "I found Sarah asleep and you gone. I had no idea what had happened to you. I had to wake up Sarah to find out where you were."

Deep in the angry brown depths of his eyes, Eloise saw concern. A tiny glow of pleasure began to grow within her. "You were honestly worried about me."

His expression darkened further. "I promised Doc Green and your mother I would see that nothing happened to you."

The glow of pleasure vanished. He was talking about duty again. "I really wish you'd get it through that thick skull of yours that I don't need you to look after me."

He raised an eyebrow. "I'm not the one in this room with the thickest skull. You must have bullied Sarah into letting you stay out here and that couldn't have been easy."

Eloise grimaced sheepishly. "I promised her I'd come in by nine. I guess she went to sleep before then."

Jonah's gaze had left her to travel over the bike parts. "What exactly are you doing with this junk?" he asked, his tone implying he thought she was wasting her time on a fool's task.

"I'm cleaning and sorting it," she replied.

He regarded her dryly. "And what do you plan to do when you've finished cleaning and sorting?"

"I plan to rebuild my bike." Eloise bit back the gasp that threatened to escape when she realized what she'd said. I've got to stop blurting out things before thinking, she admonished herself. Jonah was sure to think she was operating one brick short of a full load now.

"Well, at least I'll know where you'll be for the next several days," he said.

She stared at him, stunned. "You actually believe I can rebuild this thing?"

He met her gaze levelly. "I learned early in our marriage never to underestimate you."

Eloise found herself grinning crookedly at his show of faith in her. A warmth suddenly appeared in the dark depths of his eyes and a tingle of delight swirled through her. Then his cool, impersonal mask returned.

"However, I think it's time for you to call it a night and get some rest," he finished, his tone making this an order.

"Yes, sure," she managed to say, finding herself wanting him to kiss her so badly a hard knot was forming in the pit of her stomach. I'm the last person he wants to kiss, she mocked herself as she rose. As proof, she glanced at him. Her breath locked in her lungs. Instead of the ice she expected to see in his eyes, there was a heat so intense it caused her legs to weaken.

The memory of the two of them in this workshop flashed into her mind. They were standing looking at each other very much as they were doing now. Then abruptly he was scooping her up into his arms and striding toward the house. There was lusty purpose on his face and a grin of excitement on hers. She drew a shaky breath and forced her mind back to the present.

The cool, impersonal mask had again descended over Jonah's features. "You go on to the house. I'll turn off the lights and lock up in here," he ordered.

Approaching him, she met his gaze levelly. "Our marriage wasn't all bad," she said, her tone daring him to deny this.

"No," he conceded. Again the heat showed in his eyes. "It had its moments." Tiredness etched itself into his features. "Go to bed, Ellie," he commanded gruffly.

The urge to invite him to come with her was so strong she could feel the words forming on the tip of her tongue. Then she recalled the way he'd turned away from her last night. She refused to make a fool of herself again. Hurriedly she brushed past him and strode to the house.

Later as she lay in bed, she again recalled the flash of memory in which he picked her up and carried her to the house. "But was it love or lust?" she asked the darkness in a hushed voice. Lust for his part, came her answer. The thought that her own feelings had gone a great deal deeper played through her mind. "Please, don't let me have been so stupid, I fell in love with him," she pleaded through clenched teeth. Then exhaustion overtook her and she slept.

Eloise sat up straight and stretched her back. Except for taking a break for lunch, she'd been working on the motorcycle all day. The going had been slow. She was pretty sure she'd never put a cycle together on her own before. Sometimes, she'd have to look at a part for a long time before she'd realized where it fitted. "He didn't have to be so darn thorough when he took it apart," she grumbled.

A thud on the door that was more like a kick than a knock interrupted her complaining. "Come in," she called out.

"I can't open the door. My hands are full," came the reply.

She recognized Jonah's voice. Just the sound of it caused excitement to stir within her. "I can't believe I'm so attracted to the man," she muttered under her breath. Brushing her hands off on the legs of her jeans, she rose and walked to the door. As he opened it, her surprise grew. The smell of pizza wafted around her and she saw he was carrying a large flat box and a six-pack of sodas.

"I figured you deserved a break from Sarah's cooking," he said, extending the pizza toward her.

Taking it, she stepped back to give him room to enter. "Thanks," she managed to say, still not totally recovered from the shock of finding him there and with dinner. Then remembering her aunt, she said,

"What about Sarah? I hope she hasn't been slaving over one of her casseroles all afternoon."

"I called her earlier in the day and told her I thought she deserved a night off. I brought her a pizza of her own and she said something about going to a movie," he replied as he put all but two of the sodas into the small refrigerator in the corner.

Studying him, Eloise sensed an uncertainty about him. "This pizza smells delicious," she said, feeling the need to say something.

"It's the vegetarian. That used to be your favorite."

Setting the box down on a clear space on the workbench, she opened it and breathed in the aroma. "I think it still is."

Heading to the sink to wash her hands, she was sure she saw a momentary glimmer of relief in his eyes. The thought that he had actually wanted to please her crossed her mind and with it came a tingle of joy. You're overreacting, she scolded herself. Hadn't he made it abundantly clear he wanted out of this marriage? And, she added, she should be relieved that was his attitude. From what she knew about him so far, he would be difficult to live with...no, he would be impossible, she corrected. That was most likely why she couldn't remember what had happened between them.

As she returned to where the pizza lay, Jonah handed her a soda. The can was cold but where his fingers brushed against hers she felt a heat that sent currents up her arm. All right! All right! So her physical attraction to him was incredibly strong, she admitted grudgingly. But the physical side was only one aspect of a lasting marriage, she argued. She'd be smart to simply send him on his way. To her chagrin, this thought brought a sharp pang of regret.

Silently she groaned at the way he so easily confused her emotions and made her feel indecisive and uncertain about what path to take. Her jaw formed a determined line. She had to learn more about him and their relationship. That was the only way she was ever going to have any peace of mind. "When I first started working on this..." She paused to nod toward the clutter in the center of the floor. "I thought my father had been the one to teach me. But it was you, wasn't it?"

As he handed her a slice of pizza, his gaze was shuttered. "You used to sit and watch me work on my Harley. Then one day, you said what I was doing looked like fun and asked me to teach you. You were a fast learner."

"I probably inherited a knack for mechanics from my father," she speculated.

"Most likely," he agreed, then turned his attention to the pizza.

Attempting to keep the conversation going, she said questioningly, "So I was a fast learner?"

"Yes," he replied with brevity, then nodded toward the slice of pizza she was holding. "We should eat before it gets cold." His voice carried a message that he preferred not to continue talking.

Again she saw the flicker of uneasiness in his eyes. He reminded her of a nervous stallion. Forcing him to converse more right now might spook him into bolting, she reasoned. Letting her hunger take control, she applied herself to eating the pizza.

A few minutes later, as he finished the last slice, she studied him covertly. Since she'd come home from the hospital, he'd avoided her company as much as possible. When that wasn't possible, he'd kept the contact short. But tonight he'd actually sought her out.

The thought that he'd decided it was time to move out and had provided the pizza as a farewell meal crossed her mind. It would probably be for the best if he did leave, she told herself. But instead of the relief she wanted to feel, again she felt a pang of regret. The urge to think of something to say to make him agree to stay was strong. She silently groaned in frustration. He made her feel so confused!

"I was wondering if you wanted some help," he said, unexpectedly breaking his silence.

She barely managed to cover her surprise. He was offering to stay... to work with her. "Sure, if you really want to," she replied, forcing an indifference into her voice to hide her delight. After all, she had her pride and until this moment, he'd made it clear he wanted to have as little to do with her as possible.

His expression hardened. "Guess you were doing good enough on your own." Picking up the empty pizza box, he headed for the door.

Mentally she kicked herself. She'd sounded too cold, too indifferent. "Actually I've been having a little trouble." Forgetting about her pride, she rushed in front of him, blocking his exit. "I don't think I've ever put a cycle together totally on my own. I could use some help."

For a moment he hesitated and she was sure he was having second thoughts about his offer. Then with a nod, he changed direction.

As they began to work, Eloise chose not to force a conversation. She berated herself for being cowardly, but she didn't want to chase him away. To pacify her pride, she reasoned that if he left, she'd never learn anything about him.

And she did learn a lot without broaching any personal topics, she admitted after a while. He was enthusiastic about his work and he was very, very capable. But what really amazed her was how patient he was. He didn't take over rebuilding the cycle but let her have the lead. If she ran into a problem or tried to attach a piece the wrong way, he quietly explained what had to be done, then let her do it.

She smiled triumphantly as she completed the motor assembly. "Done," she announced proudly. Glancing up she saw Jonah grinning back and a sense of completeness seemed to blanket her. "What now?" she heard herself asking softly. Again a sense of déjà vu swept through her as she uttered the words. In her mind's eye she saw him leaning down and kissing her.

His gaze jerked away from her to the partially assembled cycle. "You attach it."

The feeling of déjà vu vanished but the memory lingered. Had he once kissed her under similar circumstances or had she just wanted him to kiss her so badly she'd envisioned it? she wondered. Staring at the motor to avoid looking at him, she was forced to face the truth. At least at one time, she'd been in love with her husband. That was the only explanation for the intensity of her reactions to him. What she did not know was if he had ever been in love with her.

Glancing at him out of the corner of her eye, she saw the hard set of his jaw. Jonah Tavish was not a man to let anyone get too close, she thought. How in the world had she ever fallen in love with him? Then she recalled the night of the storm and how he'd stayed with her so she wouldn't be frightened. And the day she'd gone riding alone, he'd come looking for her to make sure she was all right. He was a good, decent man, she admitted. And considering the way he was determinedly paying her back all the money she'd loaned him, he was also a proud, honest man. He was, she concluded, a man worth loving.

But he's not in love with me. This thought suddenly blazed in her mind like a neon light. It was something every fiber of her being told her was true. Hot tears of disappointment suddenly burned at the back of her eyes. Pride held them in check.

She forced her full concentration on the motor. But when she tried to move it, it proved to be awkward and heavy.

"Here, let me help," Jonah said. His shoulder brushed against her and his fingers touched hers as he sought a hold.

Each point of contact sent a current of excitement surging through her. She stared down at the motor and took a deep breath in an attempt to control the desire flaming to life within her. Just when she felt she had her emotions in check, he was forced to lean further toward her. His face was near her neck and as his warm breath teased her hair and played against her sensitive skin, she thought she was going to scream out of sheer frustration.

Stopping abruptly when the motor was barely an inch off the floor, he lowered it back down. Then releasing it, he straightened. "It's nearly eleven," he said. "I think we should call it a night. I'll help you with this in the morning."

As she, too, straightened, she looked up into his face. The desire she saw in his eyes matched her own. "Jonah?" she spoke his name in a soft, questioning voice.

His jaw tensed. The realization that she knew that look shook her. He'd been having a debate with himself and had reached a conclusion.

"My coming in here tonight was a mistake," he said gruffly. "Our marriage was a mistake."

A hard knot formed in her stomach. There was a finality in his voice that told her his mind was set. Pride ordered her to turn away and leave but something deep inside refused to obey. "Why is your being here a mistake? And why was our marriage a mistake?" she demanded.

He frowned as if angry with himself and impatient with her obtuseness. "We're from two different worlds. I could never fit into yours and I'd never ask you to fit into mine."

"That sounds like a cliché from a soap opera," she argued. "A very bad soap opera."

"It's reality," he growled back. His jaw twitched from his attempt to control his temper. He pointed to the scar on his cheek. "You don't remember how I got this. Well, I'll remind you. I got it in a bar fight in New Orleans when I was nineteen. I killed a man in that fight. He came at me with a knife and managed to cut me across the cheek. I shoved him back. He fell against the bar crookedly and snapped his neck. I served a year and a half in prison for manslaughter."

The thought of him being cut caused responding pain in her own cheek. Outrage filled her. "You were defending yourself. They had no right to put you in jail."

"It was a lesson in how not to choose my friends," he replied frostily. His gaze bored into her. "A person is judged by the company they keep. If others in this town, your mother or stepfather or the Thompsons, for instance, found out about my prison record they'd be sure to put their own spin on the story and you could find yourself ostracized from those you wanted to call friends."

Maybe it had been the discovery of his prison record that was causing her memory to block, she reasoned. "When did I find out about your past?"

His shoulders squared at the implication he'd withheld this information from her. "I told you before we were married."

Well, that couldn't be what her mind was trying so hard not to remember, she concluded. Her gaze leveled on him. "Obviously I wasn't concerned about it."

"No, you weren't," he admitted. "And that did surprise me. When I told you, I figured you'd hightail it away from me like a rabbit running from a fox. But you didn't. You said your offer remained firm."

Eloise continued to regard him narrowly. "And apparently, at that time, you weren't concerned about my reputation being tarnished by association." A bitter thought crossed her mind. "Or was getting my money so important to you, you didn't care what it would cost me and now that you have what you want you're feeling more magnanimous?"

He scowled at this accusation. "When I first married you, I figured you knew what you were doing. I'd always thought of you as a tough-minded business-woman who could take care of herself. I figured if anyone did find out about my past, you'd simply claim you didn't know anything and walk away. But you weren't what I expected. You're a decent woman."

"Was I a boring wife?" The question burst out before she could stop it. Then she heard herself adding, "Is that why you find dissolving our marriage so easy?"

He drew a terse breath. "You were never boring. I'm simply doing what I know is right for both of us." He nodded at the door. "Now go inside and I'll lock up out here."

She wanted to ask how he could be so sure about what was right for both of them but the words stuck in her throat. He knew what was right for him and that was what mattered. She wouldn't hold on to someone who didn't want to be held on to.

Jerking her gaze away from him, she left. All the time she showered, she tried to push him out of her mind, but those brown eyes of his so filled with desire haunted her. "Some men," she thought frustratedly, "can carry honor too far."

Lying in her bed, she heard footsteps coming up the stairs. She knew they belonged to Jonah because she'd heard her aunt snoring when she'd come in. She also realized she'd been lying there listening for some sound to assure her that he was in the house. Grumbling at herself for feeling a need for him to be there, she closed her eyes and slept.

Chapter Nine

The next morning Eloise came down to breakfast to discover Jonah had already eaten and left.

"He'd cooked himself some eggs and was eating when I came down," Sarah said, watching her niece closely. "You two didn't have a fight, did you?"

"No." Acting on an impulse, Eloise headed to the back door, "I forgot something in the workshop last night. I'll be right back."

Out there she discovered the reason Jonah had come in so late. He'd stayed behind and mounted the motor. "Just to avoid working with me," she muttered under her breath. The thought that it would be easiest on both of them if she simply packed his things and had them waiting on the front porch when he came home played through her mind. "And that's exactly what I'm going to do," she announced to the skeleton bike.

This decision caused a knot of pain deep inside but she determinedly ignored it.

"Did you find what you were looking for?" Sarah asked when Eloise returned to the kitchen.

"Jonah mounted the motor himself so he wouldn't have to work with me," Eloise replied bluntly. "And since he's made it clear he'd rather avoid my company, I've decided the time has come to move him out of this house," she finished. "When he gets home tonight he's going to find his things waiting for him on the front porch."

"Well, you'll need your energy so sit down and eat," Sarah ordered.

Eloise experienced a nudge of disappointment and realized she'd half hoped her aunt would try to talk her out of throwing Jonah out. "I was under the impression you like Jonah," she heard herself saying.

"I do. But you have to make your own decisions." Sarah motioned toward the table. "Sit. I've made you oatmeal with raisins, nuts and cinnamon."

"I hate oatmeal. I've always hated oatmeal," Eloise muttered.

Sarah smiled brightly. "Sounds like your memory is returning."

Elation swept through Eloise. "Yes, it does." Forgetting about the oatmeal, she searched for other revelations but there was only blankness. "Apparently my distaste for oatmeal was just a flash," she said disappointedly.

Sarah gave her an encouraging hug. "You'll remember everything in time," she said confidently, then her expression became stern. "However, oatmeal is healthy. It's a shame you couldn't have had a little quirk in your circuits and remembered liking it. Either way, you're going to eat it.''

Knowing that arguing would be useless, Eloise sat down and forced a spoonful into her mouth. Actually it didn't taste bad, she admitted, swallowing a second spoonful.

As she poured herself a cup of coffee and sat down with her niece, a thoughtful expression came over Sarah's features. "You know," she said, "Jonah reminds me of a man I once nursed."

"That must have been a harrowing experience," Eloise returned dryly.

Ignoring her niece's sarcasm, Sarah continued. "He was a stuntman for the movies and television. He'd gotten several bones broken doing some sort of jump from a helicopter. I'd never met anyone like him. Nothing seemed to frighten him. He showed me clips of some of his best work. In one he'd let spiders crawl all over him. You know, those big hairy ones."

Eloise shivered. "I get the picture."

"I asked him how he could do all those things," Sarah said.

When her aunt suddenly became silent, Eloise looked up. "And what did he say?"

Sarah's gaze leveled on Eloise. "He said the trick was not to care. He said he couldn't get hurt if he didn't care."

For a long moment Eloise just sat staring into her aunt's face. Buds of memory began to sprout. They weren't totally coherent. They were more flashes than full scenes. Abruptly she pushed back her chair and rose. "I think I need to go sit on the porch for a while and think," she said.

"You go do that," Sarah called to her departing back.

Sitting in the porch swing, Eloise began to remember a great many things. Some were good and some were bad.

One thing, however, did puzzle her. Reflecting on when she and Jonah had gotten married, she recalled that Reverend Randal had voiced no objections to the match. At the time, the Reverend was fairly new in town. He'd only been in Hornsburg for a couple of years and she'd assumed that his lack of cautionary advice to the match was because he knew neither her nor Jonah well and simply had no opinion. Or, perhaps he knew her well enough to know she was going to do whatever she wanted to do regardless of his advice and didn't want to offend her and possibly lose her contributions to the church.

But when he'd come to visit her in the hospital, Jonah had been in her room. The reverend had shaken Jonah's hand and his manner toward her husband had been openly friendly. This had left her with the impression that the reverend knew Jonah and honestly liked him.

"You want some help packing Jonah's things?"

Eloise looked to the door to find Sarah standing there obviously ready for action. "I've decided to reconsider that decision," she replied.

"Then I'll just get back to my baking," Sarah said, and went back inside.

Eloise grimaced crookedly at the now empty doorway. "She's agreed to everything, other than the oatmeal, I've said this morning and managed to leave me with nothing but doubts."

Scooting off the porch swing, she went inside and found her purse and keys. Then she sought out Sarah. "I've begun remembering a few things. One of them is how to drive. I'm going into town."

"I'll expect you back in time for lunch," Sarah replied, her tone making this an order. "If you're going to be late, call or I'll have Jonah and the sheriff out looking for you."

Eloise gave her aunt a reassuring hug. "Don't worry. I'll be fine."

A little later she was sitting in Reverend Randal's office facing him across his desk.

"It's good to see you up and about," he said.

She knew he'd noticed that she'd closed the door when she came in and, behind his polite expression, she read the curiosity in his eyes. "Some of my memory has returned," she said.

He smiled warmly. "I'm glad to hear that."

She fought down the urge to fidget. "But what I do remember has raised a couple of questions."

"Go on," he encouraged when she hesitated.

Her nervousness grew. "I don't want to offend you but there is no subtle way to say what I have to say."

"I'll be sure to turn the other cheek," he replied.

Eloise's back tensed. "When Jonah and I came to ask you to marry us, you didn't attempt to counsel us in any way. At the time I assumed you were simply indifferent, that your only interest in me was as a wealthy member of your congregation who donated a substantial amount each year and that you did not want to antagonize me."

He smiled to let her know he wasn't offended. "I didn't attempt to counsel either of you because you were both people who had always held your own counsel. And I trusted both of you to know what was best for you."

Eloise frowned. "But how did you know you could trust Jonah? I'm certain he never attended this church or any other before we were married. And, from the bits I do remember, I feel certain he never attended after we were married."

"That's true," he confirmed.

"And what puzzles me even more," she hurried on, "is the way you behaved when you came to visit me in the hospital. Jonah was there and the way you greeted him gave me the impression that you knew him. Actually it was more than that. I had the feeling you not only knew him, but you liked him."

The reverend's smile faded and his expression became somber. "It would be more correct to say I know of your husband rather than to say I know him personally."

A plea entered Eloise's voice. "I need to make some decisions and I need to know what you know."

Reverend Randal sat back in his chair and studied her thoughtfully. "I suppose there is no ethical reason for me not to tell you. In ministering to some of the less fortunate in town, I discovered that your husband has been a benefactor to quite a few."

Eloise stared at him in surprise. "Jonah?"

"He's kept old Earl Stanson's truck going for the past several years for the price of a meal every once in a while or a fresh-baked pie."

"I remember he'd bring home a pie or cake or a jar of honey every once in a while and say it was from a satisfied customer." She recalled her visit to Jonah's garage earlier in the week. Tommy had mentioned Jonah was out helping old Mrs. Lester and that the woman would probably bring some homemade cookies by the next day. Now she realized that was probably all the payment Jonah would accept from the elderly woman.

"I've had people tell me that when they were having hard times, sometimes there'd be a knock on their door after dark and they'd go and find a basket filled with food," the reverend continued. "In a couple of cases there was money in there, too. Old Mrs. Jarvis, she keeps an eye on everything and everybody, she told me she'd seen Jonah leaving a basket or two. But we both agree that since he didn't seem to want anyone to know, we'd keep it our secret. The people he helped were proud people who would've felt they owed him a favor and she and I guessed he didn't want that."

Eloise nodded in agreement. Jonah wouldn't want anything from anyone.

"Then there's Tommy Dunn," Reverend Randal added. "Jonah took the boy under his wing and protected him."

Another bit of memory flashed into Eloise's mind. "And Jonah plans to help him get through college."

The reverend leaned on his desk to bring himself closer to her. "I made a point of going by and speaking to Jonah one day. I wanted to thank him for the aid he'd given. He told me he was doing it because of a promise he'd made Clyde Gilder. He said Clyde had asked him to do a good deed once in a while in Clyde's memory." The reverend leaned even closer. "But if you want my opinion, Jonah Tavish is a good man and he does those deeds because he wants to do them and not just because he's keeping a promise."

"I appreciate you telling me this," she said.

He studied her thoughtfully. "I hope I've been able to help."

"You have," she replied. "You've confirmed some things my instincts have been telling me."

"If you'd like to talk about this decision you feel you need to make, I'm here to listen," he offered.

Rising, she extended her hand to him. "As you said, I'm used to keeping my own counsel."

Accepting her handshake, he gave her an encouraging smile. "If you should change your mind, my door's always open."

"Thank you," she replied and left.

Driving back to the farm, Jonah filled her mind. As she had told the reverend, her memory wasn't complete. But she had remembered that she'd desperately wanted her marriage to work. And the reverend's revelations simply served to confirm her belief that her husband was a man worth loving.

"He doesn't have any better prospects than me so he might as well stay with me," she reasoned, her jaw set with resolve.

The reverend's information also gave her hope that the hard shell Jonah kept around his heart wasn't as impenetrable as she'd begun to believe. But even if he never allowed himself to fully open his heart to her, she didn't care. She wanted to share her life with him and until he had someplace better to go, she was going to do what she could to keep him with her.

"You look like a woman with a purpose," Sarah observed when Eloise walked into the kitchen.

"I've decided to keep my husband," Eloise replied.

Sarah grinned. "A bird in the hand is worth two in the bush."

"Jonah's more of a snarling dog than a bird in hand, but he's worth the challenge," Eloise returned.

Sarah studied her. "Your memory is coming back."

"It's still just bits and pieces. But I do know I want my marriage to work," Eloise replied.

"Then I'm sure you'll find a way," Sarah said with confidence.

Eloise gave her aunt a hug. Then going to the refrigerator, she began pulling out food. "I'm going to pack a lunch and take it to Jonah. He's going to discover I'm not that easy to avoid."

A little later, with the lunch on the seat beside her and the bent fender and wheel from her bike in her trunk, she arrived at Jonah's gas station.

"I thought you were going to spend the day working on your bike," he said, coming out of one of the bays.

"I am," she replied, ignoring the edge of impatience in his voice. "You promised me you'd help get the dents out of my fender and I need the wheel repaired."

"Just leave them. I'll take care of them as soon as I finish with the car I'm working on."

Before she could even respond, he started walking back into the garage. "You're not going to get rid of me that easily," she murmured under her breath to his departing back.

Following him inside, she approached the car on which he was working. Standing close beside him as he peered under the hood, she brushed her shoulder against his as she leaned over to peer with him. "What's wrong with it?"

"Don't know yet. It keeps stalling. Probably a problem with the choke," he replied coolly.

She shifted closer to him until her hip rested against his. "Where's the choke?"

"Where you can't see it," he returned with curt impatience.

Her resolve weakened. Maybe the real reason he was so intent on ending their marriage was that he was bored with being married and honestly wanted out. She wouldn't keep him against his will.

"You're standing a little too close," he grumbled. "I need more elbow room."

The words to tell him her memory was returning and he could leave any time he wanted with a free conscience formed on the tip of her tongue.

Then she saw the spark of desire flare in his eyes. Immediately he jerked his attention back to the engine.

Her resolve returned. Where there's a spark, a fire can start, she mused silently. Then mentally laughed at herself. She was beginning to sound like Sarah.

Obediently she shifted a little away from him. "I brought some lunch."

"Thanks." He dropped the tool he'd been holding and cursed under his breath at his clumsiness.

Realizing he was rattled by her presence, Eloise had to fight to keep from smiling. It'd be best not to push too hard too fast, she cautioned herself.

Forcing herself to leave him alone for a little while, she straightened and walked back outside. She did, however, make sure she added a little extra swing to her hips. A prickling sensation on the back of her neck caused her to glance over her shoulder. He was watching her and she was sure she saw heat in his eyes. Immediately he returned his attention to the car. So far, so good, she told herself encouragingly as she opened the trunk and took out the fender and wheel.

It was hard staying away from him. Just looking at him gave her pleasure. Touching him caused a rush of excitement. I'm like a bee drawn to honey, metal drawn to a magnet, an idiot on a fool's errand. She scowled at herself and tossed out this last analogy. If she won him, the reward would be worth the risk.

"Hi."

Eloise jerked around at the sound of the friendly greeting to discover Tommy approaching.

"Had to run over and jump start the mayor's car. He'd left the headlights on all night," he said. His gaze fell on the fender and wheel. "Those look like pieces of your bike."

"They are. I brought them in to get them repaired." A part of her was glad the boy was there. His presence would force her to be subtle. Another part, though, wanted Jonah all to herself. I am really crazy about that man, she admitted, the extent of her feelings causing her to feel shaky.

"Let me help you." Picking up the wheel and fender, Tommy carried them into the second bay. "The wheel didn't get bent. So all you'll need is a new tire," he said after a quick examination. "But the fender's going to take a little pounding to put it right."

A bell sounded signaling that someone was pulling into the line of full-service pumps.

"Got a customer," Tommy said apologetically, and hurried out.

Unable to stay away from Jonah any longer, Eloise slowly, as if simply wandering aimlessly, returned to his side. Again she stood close enough to him to brush her body against his as she feigned interest in his work. "How's it coming?"

"Since you're obviously feeling so much better, don't you think the polite thing for you to do would be to take your aunt sight-seeing?" he suggested.

She noticed that he didn't look up at her. She also heard the gruff edge in his voice. It was a gruffness she recognized . . . one that had nothing to do with anger. Again she had to fight to keep from grinning.

The bell inside the service station rang announcing a customer who had pumped his own gas and now wanted to pay. She noticed Tommy was still busy. "Aunt Sarah seemed perfectly happy being left on her own. I'll go take care of that customer."

As before, she made certain she gave her hips an extra swing while walking away and, as before, she experienced a prickling sensation on the back of her neck. Glancing over her shoulder, she again caught him looking at her. This time there was no mistaking the heat in his gaze. Quickly he returned his attention to the engine. Slipping in behind the cash register, she grinned. This little game of seduction was stimulating and a whole lot of fun.

It was also frustrating, she added as she took the picnic basket out of the car a couple of hours later. With customers and Tommy constantly around, she'd been forced to keep her flirting discreet. No nibbling on his earlobe, she'd had to order herself, when the urge had been close to overwhelming.

But now she hoped to get Jonah alone for a while.

"Jonah asked me to join you two for lunch," Tommy said, coming to help her. "I told him I didn't mind eating what I had in the fridge but he insisted."

Eloise fought back a groan. "I did bring along enough for ten people," she admitted, recalling how she'd begun throwing food in and hadn't been able to stop herself until Sarah had asked if she planned to feed the entire town. "You're more than welcome to join us," she forced herself to add out of politeness.

This wasn't how she'd pictured her lunch with Jonah, she grumbled silently a few minutes later as she sat at the picnic table under a tree to the side of the station eating her sandwich while the man and boy discussed the finer points of adjusting chokes. A car pulled up to the self-service pump and she volunteered to collect the customer's money.

Leaving the table, she wondered if Jonah would even notice her absence. Then she again experienced the prickling at the back of her neck. Out of the corner of her eye, she saw him looking her way. A crooked smile tilted one corner of her mouth as she waited on the customer.

A little later as she was repacking the uneaten food and insisting that Tommy keep the leftovers, she decided that remaining here at the station would prove to be more frustrating than productive.

"I think I should go check on Sarah," she said to Jonah when Tommy went to put the leftovers in his apartment.

"Sounds like a good idea to me," he replied approvingly.

She would have felt piqued except that she was determined to believe her presence had him so rattled he hadn't been able to entirely concentrate on his work. He had two more cars waiting for repairs and the job he'd been working on when she'd arrived had taken him a lot longer than it should have.

"See you at dinner." She stopped herself from placing a light kiss on his lips. She didn't want to frighten him away. He'd made it clear he intended to keep his distance and he wasn't a man who was going to easily allow himself to be dissuaded from his stated goal.

Back at the farm, she busied herself rebuilding her bike. She'd left the fender at the garage. Tommy had gotten a couple of dents out of it but it still needed some work. As for the wheel, Tommy had put a new tire on it and she'd brought that back with her. She'd just finished mounting it when a knock on the door was followed by Mark Thompson's entrance.

"I can't believe you're fixing that...that thing," he growled. "It almost killed you."

"The accident was my fault," she corrected.

He shrugged as if whose fault it was didn't matter. "My mother called to tell me she saw you working at Jonah's gas station. You're supposed to be resting."

His patronizing manner grated on her nerves but she ordered herself to be polite. "I rested for weeks in the hospital. Besides I wasn't working. I'd just stopped by to take him lunch and I helped out when they had a rush of customers."

Mark drew a terse breath. "You're thinking of staying with him, aren't you?"

"He's my husband."

Crossing the room in long strides, he captured her by the upper arms. "I should have been your husband. Everyone expected us to get married. I was the logical choice."

Jerking free, she took a step back. "I married the man I wanted."

Fury etched itself into Mark's face. "You'll wake up one morning and discover all your money and your precious 'husband' gone."

She regarded him levelly. "You're wrong. That won't happen."

"Someday you'll regret the choice you made," he warned.

As he stalked out, slamming the door behind him, a shiver ran along Eloise's spine. More memories returned. "He's been spoilt by his mother and his father," she reasoned aloud. "He's just blowing off steam...throwing a tantrum." She'd seen him lose his temper before. That was another trait of his that had made her question her desire to marry him. When he'd had time to cool down, he'd regret getting angry and come back and apologize.

Pushing Mark out of her mind, she returned her attention to the bike. It was looking pretty good, she thought. Jonah would be proud of her. Doubts suddenly assailed her. Was she doing the right thing by trying to make their marriage work? I'm a good wife for him, she told herself firmly. And I won't try to hold him if he honestly wants to leave.

Glancing at the clock, she gasped and practically ran for the house. On her way home that afternoon, she'd bought the ingredients for Jonah's favorite dinner and when she'd returned home, she'd informed Sarah she would be cooking tonight. She'd made the chili before coming out to work on the bike, leaving Sarah with strict orders her aunt was only to stir it occasionally and not add anything. When she'd issued this command, she'd been worried about hurting Sarah's feelings but her aunt had merely smiled knowingly.

Now, taking the steps two at a time, Eloise judged she had just enough time to clean up and get the corn bread into the oven before Jonah was due home.

All afternoon, she'd mentally reviewed her wardrobe. Finally she settled on the blue-checkered cotton dress with a scoop neck and a full skirt. It was fastened with buttons down the front and she recalled one evening when Jonah had seemed to particularly enjoy himself slowly unfastening each one. As she dressed, she also recalled that she'd enjoyed that evening very much as well.

"I'm afraid I have some disheartening news," Sarah said when Eloise came downstairs. "Jonah called while you were in the shower."

"He's got too much work to do and he's going to get something from a fast-food place for dinner," she finished for her aunt.

Sarah nodded. "I told him you'd fixed chili and that I hadn't done anything but stir it. For a minute I thought he was going to change his mind, then he said, he'd have some when he got home and hung up." She gave her niece a sympathetic look. "I'm sorry."

"You did your best," Eloise assured her. Her back straightened with resolve. "I'm determined to believe he's attempting to avoid me because he's afraid I might break through that stone wall around his heart," she stated as much for her own ears as for her aunt's.

Sarah smiled. "I've seen the way he behaves when he thinks you're in danger. It's my opinion that wall is very close to crumbling."

Eloise gave her aunt a hug. "Thanks, I needed to hear that." She grimaced apologetically. "I'm going to leave you to eat alone. He's going to learn I'm not easy to get rid of."

"I'd have pushed you out the door myself, if you hadn't decided to go on your own," Sarah replied, giving her a nudge toward the door.

Driving to Jonah's garage, Eloise reached up and unbuttoned the top button of her dress. The effect pleased her. It allowed a bit of cleavage to show and added a definite sexy touch.

Jonah was in one of the bays. He had a car up on the rack and was under it working on the exhaust system. The Closed sign was on the door and Tommy was nowhere around. She recalled he'd found a girlfriend and guessed he'd already left to go see her.

At least Jonah and I will be alone, she thought. Joining her husband beneath the vehicle, she saw the look of surprise on his face. Then his gaze dipped to her cleavage and heat sparked in his eyes. Jerking his attention back to the exhaust system, he said stiffly, "Sorry I couldn't make it home in time for dinner."

"It's the dessert you should be sorry you missed," she replied.

He looked back at her, his expression grim. "I thought we'd both agreed it'd be smart if we didn't continue our marriage."

A thought that had been nagging at the back of her mind caused a hard knot in her stomach. "Do you have a better prospect? Is there someone else you'd rather be married to?"

"No, there isn't anyone else." His jaw tensed with purpose. "I thought I'd already told you I don't believe in love or any of that everlasting nonsense."

"You did mention that," she admitted, the knot in her stomach untying.

He'd returned his attention to the exhaust system to signal an end to their conversation. She frowned up at him. "You might be able to intimidate others into leaving you alone but you can't intimidate me, Jonah Tavish."

His expression shuttered, he again looked down at her.

"I had planned to have this conversation dressed in my red silk nightie," she confessed bluntly. "However, that really isn't suitable for public display."

"You're dressed just fine," he assured her gruffly.

Again she saw the heat in his eyes before he was able to mask it. Her courage buoyed, she continued. "*We* didn't agree the smartest move would be to dissolve our marriage. I admit you can be stubborn, authoritarian and downright difficult to get along with at times but that doesn't seem to bother me too much. I've learned that your bark is worse than your bite."

"Careful. You're beginning to sound like Aunt Sarah," he cautioned dryly.

She merely frowned up at him. "No amount of sarcasm is going to change my mind. My instincts tell me you're a good man, Jonah, and I'm following them."

His jaw twitched and she had the impression he was having an inner struggle with himself. Hoping the battle would come out in her favor, she continued levelly, "I've gotten used to having you around and I want you to stay." Her gaze locked onto his. "And I want you back in my bed."

She'd planned on making this little speech in his bedroom and she'd envisioned herself disrobing him while she talked. But with the bay door open and cars passing in the street, her thoughts of seducing him on the spot were stymied. "Think about what I've said," she finished. "I'm going home and putting on that red silk nightie."

Striding back to her car, her legs felt rubbery. What if he didn't follow her home? Glancing in her rear-view mirror as she pulled out into the street, she saw him still standing where she'd left him. She did note he hadn't returned to working on the exhaust system. Instead he was watching her.

Leaving town, she was forced to take one hand off the wheel at a time to dry her sweaty palms. Again she wondered what she would do if he didn't come. Again her stomach knotted.

"If he doesn't come this time, I'll try again," she told herself. "Some nuts are harder to crack than others." She shook her head at herself. She was truly beginning to sound like her aunt.

Sarah was sitting in the porch swing when Eloise arrived home. "Is Jonah coming to dinner after all?" she asked as Eloise mounted the steps.

"If he does come, it'd better not be for the chili," Eloise replied.

Sarah's eyes glistened with amusement as she rose. "Then I'll go put it in the refrigerator. You two can reheat it later if you need nourishment."

"Thanks," Eloise replied, continuing on up the stairs. Twice during the drive home she'd seen headlights in her rearview mirror but both times the cars had turned off. With each step she took, her fear that he wouldn't follow her home increased. By the time she had changed into the silk nightgown, she was being besieged by doubts.

Turning off her lights, she walked over to the window and stared out at the night. She'd promised herself that if she failed tonight, she'd try again but she wasn't so sure she would keep that promise. She had her pride.

A tear of frustration trickled down her cheek. Damn his determined isolationist attitude, she cursed silently. Suddenly the flash of headlights in the distance caught her attention. A vehicle was coming up the driveway. By the sound of its engine, she knew it was Jonah's truck even before it was close enough for her to see clearly.

She watched him enter the house. Hearing his footsteps on the stairs, she turned to her door. But he didn't come her way. Instead she heard him turn down the hall in the other direction. Her hands fastened around the back of the chair beside her as she fought to control the hurt. A couple of minutes later, she heard the shower running in the guest bathroom.

Sarah was still on the porch. Eloise knew that because of the squeak of the porch swing. Releasing the chair, she paced the floor. He had been pretty grimy. Maybe he was cleaning up before he came to her room, she reasoned. Or maybe he'd opted for a cold shower so he wouldn't have to worry about that shell of his being cracked, her pessimistic side insisted on adding.

She heard the water being turned off. In her mind's eye she visualized how good he looked when he stepped out of his shower. A fire ignited within her. But it was the memory of the tender way he touched her that caused the flames to rise, threatening to consume her. The first time they'd made love, she had been surprised by how gentle and considerate he'd been. At other times he'd exhibited an unexpected playfulness.

Her body tensed as she strained to hear his footsteps in the hall. Her jaw trembled with relief when she heard them coming her way. Still, her body remained rigid with fear he might suddenly change his mind.

She heard him come to a halt outside her door. Standing frozen, she watched the knob. It turned and the door opened. In the light from the hall, she saw him standing there. He was wearing only a pair of jeans. She couldn't do anything but look at him. The sight of him, bare chested and barefoot, had always aroused her but never more than now.

Entering, he closed the door. Moonlight filtering in through the windows softly illuminated the room. He didn't say anything as he approached her. But when he drew her into his arms and his mouth found hers the hunger in his kiss told her he'd been missing her as much as she'd been missing him.

"I hope when your memory returns, you won't regret this," he growled against her lips.

"I can assure you I won't," she replied.

His hands had traveled exploringly down her back then lower to cup the fullness of her buttocks. Her legs weakened. Wrapping her arms around his neck she fitted her body against his. The sense of being exactly where she belonged pervaded every fiber of her being.

His mouth left hers to trail kisses along the sensitive cord of her neck.

Issuing a purr of pleasure she nuzzled her face against his hair-matted chest. Then loosening her hold, she eased away from him just far enough to allow herself to find the buckle of his jeans.

His hands moved to her hips as he gave her room to work. "You're definitely the sexiest accountant I've ever known," he murmured in her ear.

"And I like the sum of your attributes," she returned, easing his zipper down.

His hands found the straps of her nightgown. "I like the feel of silk but I like the feel of you better," he admitted huskily.

"My sentiments, too," she murmured against his skin. Straightening away from him, she allowed him to slip the straps off her shoulders and stood as the garment slowly dropped to the floor.

Once free, she reached for his jeans and helped him out of them. The sturdy columns of his legs brought a smile to her lips and she trailed her hand upward along his thigh as she moved into his arms once again.

"It's been too long," he growled. "I need you now."

There had been no necessity for him to tell her, she thought, feeling a womanly power so strong she came close to giving a yell of triumph. "I need you, too," she assured him, drawing him to the bed.

As he claimed her, she trembled with pleasure. This was where she belonged, she thought with confidence. Still she could not relax until she was certain he was as satisfied with their joining as she was. Then releasing herself to the pure joy of uniting with him, she let the fires of passion consume her.

Later as she lay beside him, Eloise felt a sliver of guilt. She should tell him her memory was returning. But fear held her back. Several times he'd said he planned to leave as soon as she was healed and she wasn't certain tonight would make him change his mind. She didn't want to keep him there if he really wanted to go but giving herself a few more days to convince him to stay couldn't hurt. And he had said he had no other prospects or anywhere better to be.

Running her hand lazily over his chest, she looked up at his face. Besides, he didn't look like a man being held against his will. And as for her memory, it wasn't entirely intact yet. Mostly only her strongest memories had returned and the majority of them revolved around Jonah. But even where he was concerned there were still gaps. She still didn't know what had made her try that wheelie. Having at least partially satisfied her conscience with this little argument, she kissed his shoulder then levered herself onto an elbow.

"I don't know about you, but I'm starved," she announced. "How about some chili?"

"From the look in your eyes, it's my guess I'm going to need nourishment," he replied in a easy drawl.

"Most assuredly," she confirmed, already feeling the embers of desire beginning to compete with her hunger.

He smiled then, amusement mingling with enjoyment in his eyes. Her heart seemed to do a flip-flop. She loved seeing him happy. "I am good for you and the sooner you let yourself admit we make a terrific pair, the better off you'll be," she told him, finishing with a kiss on the tip of his nose.

Reaching up, he gently combed a lock of hair off her forehead. "You could be right."

Her breath locked in her lungs. He'd come to within an inch of agreeing with her. "I know I am," she said with conviction.

He studied her. "That knock on the head has changed you. You used to keep your own counsel. You never said what was on your mind."

An anxiousness swept through her. "Does my openness bother you?"

"No," he admitted after a moment. "I used to wonder what you were thinking. Now I don't have to."

Hope grew. "You actually wondered about me and what I was thinking?"

An uneasiness flickered in his eyes. "I like to know where I stand."

She was tempted to ask him where she stood but the words refused to be spoken. Coward, she berated herself, admitting she couldn't bear to hear him tell her politely that she was pleasant company but that was as far as it went. Her stomach growled. "Food. We need food," she said, quickly slipping out of bed and finding her robe.

In the hall, she heard the faint sound of the television in Sarah's bedroom. Obviously her aunt had retired for the night. Discreetly getting herself out of the way, Eloise thought, grateful to Sarah for being so diplomatic.

She'd just gotten the chili out of the refrigerator and was spooning some into a pan to heat when Jonah joined her. He'd only taken the time to pull on his jeans. Her gaze rested on his broad shoulders then traveled to his hard flat abdomen. A thrill raced through her. She shifted her attention to his face. Suddenly she was remembering the intoxicatingly rough texture of his jaw early in the morning before he shaved. And she recalled how much she'd loved just lying beside him, watching him sleep. The thought that she could get badly hurt shook her. Abruptly she shoved it out of her mind. She would not let fear stop her from pursuing him.

"That chili's going to burn if you don't turn the heat down," he cautioned.

She flushed and quickly turned her attention to the stove. He makes me feel like a teenager in heat, she thought, fighting down the urge to ease her way into his arms that very minute.

Coming up behind her, he ruffled her hair and kissed her lightly on the side of the neck. "I have missed being with you," he said gruffly in her ear.

Her heart pounded so loudly she was sure he could hear it. First he'd admitted to thinking about her and now he'd admitted to having missed her. Maybe she was breaking through that hard crust he kept around himself. Turning to him, she grinned up at him. "This dinner is in grave danger of being burned."

Laughing lightly, he bent to kiss her. Just as their lips met, her stomach growled loudly. Giving her only a light peck, he stepped back. "I think we'd better get some food into you."

She grimaced self-consciously. "Maybe so."

Abruptly his expression became grimly serious. Cupping her face in his hands, he looked hard into her eyes. "I want your word you won't ever again try a stunt like the one that landed you in the hospital. It scared the hell out of me."

Behind the protectiveness in his eyes, she was sure she saw real fear. Maybe she had truly pierced that shell of his. "I promise."

He nodded with satisfaction. An uneasiness suddenly shadowed his features and his expression became shuttered. "I'll set the table," he said, releasing her and quickly turning to the cabinet that held the dishes.

I may have broken through but he's not ready to admit it, she thought disappointedly. Watching him, she knew he was attempting to rebuild his protective wall. I just hope he doesn't have regrets and reconstruct it even stronger, she prayed silently.

Again a feeling of déjà vu filled her. There had been other times when she'd thought she'd broken through his wall, she realized. Her stomach knotted as more memories burst forth. She'd never succeed in maintaining the breach.

Glancing over her shoulder at him as he set the table, she was forced to admit her goal might be unattainable. But she wasn't ready to give up yet, not when they'd come so far. Feeling even more determined, she turned her attention back to the chili.

Chapter Ten

"Well, I'm glad to see the two of you looking so mellow," Sarah said.

It was the next morning and Eloise was seated across the table from Jonah lazily watching him over the rim of her coffee cup. "Yes, it is," she replied absently.

Rising from her seat, Sarah walked toward the coffeepot. Halfway there, she paused and looked back. "As long as I'm up, do either of you want anything else to eat? I've got more hot cereal," she offered. "Guess putting those apples and dates in the oatmeal was just the right combination. Of course, it could have been that touch of vanilla."

Eloise looked down to discover she'd finished her bowl of oatmeal. Jonah had eaten his, too, in addition to an omelet with a mixture of ingredients neither wanted to question Sarah about. She smiled softly. They'd both been too hungry to care what the food tasted like. "Thanks but I'm stuffed," Eloise replied.

Jonah nodded. "Me, too."

"You both look a little tired today," Sarah observed, continuing to regard them thoughtfully. "Maybe you should have slept in."

Jonah grinned mischievously at Eloise. "I think I'll get more rest going to work," he said huskily.

Sarah laughed and continued to the coffeepot to pour herself another cup.

The thought of trying to convince Jonah to spend the day with her played through Eloise's mind. Ever since she'd woken this morning, she'd been hating the thought of being separated from him. Don't push too hard too fast, she cautioned herself for the umpteenth time. Still, she heard herself saying, "Maybe you should take the morning off."

His jaw suddenly tensed. "I've got a business to run."

She saw the pride flash in his eyes. He was reminding her that even if he was married to a wealthy woman, he wasn't a man of leisure. "I'll bring lunch," she volunteered quickly, letting him know she understood and respected his decision.

His grin returned. "You're too much of a distraction. I've got work to catch up on from yesterday and I don't want to be late for dinner. I'll take a sandwich."

Give him room, she ordered herself. "As long as you promise not to be late," she bargained already on her way to make his sandwich.

"I promise," he replied in an easy drawl.

An underlying note in his voice let her know that again they wouldn't be getting a lot of sleep. Her toes curled with anticipation as she finished packing his lunch.

The sound of a car coming up the driveway caused Eloise to glance out the window. A groan issued.

Jonah looked over her shoulder and scowled. "What's Mark Thompson doing here this early?"

Causing trouble, Eloise thought, watching a coolness descend over Jonah's features. "I'll find out," she said, heading for the front door. Hoping to get rid of Mark quickly, she stepped out onto the porch as he came up the steps.

"I wanted to apologize for yesterday afternoon. I lost my temper and said a few things I shouldn't have," he said, shoving a huge bouquet of flowers into her arms. "I made my uncle get up and open his shop early just so I could bring these to you. I remembered how much you used to love orchids."

A prickling on the back of her neck caused Eloise to glance over her shoulder. Jonah was standing in the doorway, his expression shuttered. "I'd really like for you to get on with your life and let me get on with mine," she said with dismissal, attempting to return the flowers.

"I want us to be friends," Mark insisted, refusing to take back the bouquet. He looked past her shoulder and she knew he'd seen Jonah. Returning his attention to her, he said firmly, "If you ever regain your senses, I'll be waiting." Then before she could respond, he left.

"Nice flowers," Jonah said, coming out onto the porch to join her. "Expensive," he added.

She looked down at the bouquet. He was right. Among the baby's breath and ferns there was mostly orchids with a few roses for variety. "He gets them at a discount," she said. Sensing the barrier Jonah kept around himself again growing strong she wanted to drop the flowers on the porch and tramp them. Instead she met his gaze levelly. "I know what I want, Jonah, and it's not Mark Thompson or his flowers. I want you."

The warmth returned to his eyes and he smiled with pleasure. She was winning! Going up on tiptoe, she kissed him lightly. "Don't be late for dinner," she ordered.

"I won't," he promised.

As he drove off, she stood on the porch watching until she could no longer see his truck. Joy filled her. She was gaining his trust and hopefully with it would come his heart. Going inside, she threw the flowers into the trash before helping Sarah clean the dishes.

"Eloise!"

A tap on the shoulder and her name being shouted in her ear caused Eloise to jerk around. As soon as she'd finished helping Sarah in the kitchen, she'd hurried out to the workshop to complete assembling her motorcycle. There had only been a couple of small tasks left. Now the bike was back in one piece except for the missing rear fender. She'd wheeled it out to the side of the workshop and was testing the engine before taking it on a practice run. Switching off the machine, she grinned up at her aunt. "As soon as I get the fender back, it'll be as good as new," she announced with pride. Her smile broadened. "I can't wait for Jonah to see it."

"Jonah's what I'm here about," Sarah said.

Reading the anxiousness in her aunt's eyes, panic swept through Eloise. "What's happened? Has he been hurt?"

The concern on Sarah's face increased. "He came home a few minutes ago. I didn't even hear him come in. I was in the kitchen and you were out here making a racket testing that engine."

"He's here?" Eloise started toward the house to find out for herself what was wrong.

Sarah caught her by the arm. "He just left. He took some of his things. He came by the kitchen to tell me he'd send Tommy for the rest."

"He left?" Eloise couldn't believe this was happening. "You have to be mistaken!"

Sarah looked as if she wanted to cry. "I wish I was. I asked him why he was leaving. He just said he should never have married you in the first place and he left."

Eloise felt as if her whole world was falling apart. A flood of memories assailed her. The day of the accident was suddenly crystal clear. "He can't leave me without a better explanation than that!" Mounting her bike, she started the engine, hit her heel against the kick stand to raise it and then took off down around the house.

Reaching the main road, she saw Jonah's truck as a distant dot ahead of her. Forgetting caution, she increased her speed. The wind whipped through her hair and tears blurred her vision as she caught up with him and went around him. In her rearview mirror she saw him slow. She signaled with a wave of her arm for him to pull over.

As he guided his truck onto a wide spot of grassy shoulder, she slowed and pulled over ahead of him.

"What the devil do you think you're doing?" he demanded, anger etched into his features as he climbed out of the cab and slammed the door so hard the truck shook. "You were riding like a maniac! A helmetless maniac to boot!" He pointed an accusing finger at the bike. "That thing's not even all together."

"It's just missing a fender," she said defensively. She'd never seen him so furious and she took a step back as he approached.

Noticing her backward movement, he came to an abrupt stop. Still glaring at her, he growled, "You should be banned from riding anything with only two wheels."

Her jaw trembled. She probably wouldn't like what she was going to hear but she had to hear it anyway. "I want to know why you're leaving."

His expression grew grimmer. "I found out the truth."

That was one answer she hadn't expected. She stared at him in confusion. "What 'truth'?"

"Thompson came by my station. He accused me of taking advantage of your loss of memory," he said coldly.

"Taking advantage of me?" she repeated, wishing she'd thrown the flowers back at Mark that morning.

"I've always wondered why you cut a deal to marry me because I needed your money but you wouldn't marry him because you thought he wanted your money. Now I understand. He told me about the affair.''

Eloise wished she could get her hands around Mark's throat at that moment. "He told you about his affair?"

"You must have been really crazy about him for that to have sent you into my arms," Jonah continued curtly. "I figure you can't remember your past because you don't want to remember how much in love with him you were. And if you're smart, you won't ever remember that part."

She saw the pain mingling with his anger. "You're jealous," she gasped, her fear of losing him being displaced by elation.

"Every man gets made a fool of once in his life," he tossed over his shoulder as he headed back to his truck.

Racing after him, she caught him by the arm. "I am *not* nor have I *ever* been in love with Mark Thompson."

He looked down at her cynically. "Don't you think you should wait until you get your memory back before you go making such rash statements?"

"I do have my memory back," she confessed. "It started coming back a couple of days ago but there were gaps. When Sarah told me you were leaving, everything came back."

He continued to regard her icily. He's building his wall again, she thought frantically. "Before I found out about Mark's affair, I'd decided I couldn't marry him. I'd tried to convince myself that he was the practical choice. But the thought of sharing my life with him left me cold. I would have broken up with him sooner but I was looking for a polite way to get rid of him. After all, his father and I are partners and I have to work with Mark. The affair, even his interest in my money, were merely excuses.''

Jonah didn't look convinced.

You're going to have to tell him everything, she ordered herself. "I couldn't get that kiss between you and me off my mind,'' she continued nervously. "I tried telling myself you and I didn't have anything in common. But you started showing up in my dreams. I've never done anything rash or even unreasonable in my life. But I couldn't stop thinking about you.''

The anger on his face had faded. His expression was still shuttered but he was listening, she told herself encouragingly. "I wanted you for my husband. When this urge first hit me, I brushed it aside as ridiculous but it kept coming back. Every time I'd see you, it grew stronger. I knew you weren't the marrying kind. And you weren't at all what I'd been looking for as a husband. Still, I couldn't get you out of my mind. Then your garage burned and I came up with the marriage proposal idea. I told myself it was crazy but I couldn't stop myself. I figured you'd toss me out and that would get you out of my system then I could go looking for someone more suitable.''

His anger returned. "It would have been best if you'd gone looking for someone more suitable from the start.''

Mentally she kicked herself. "That didn't come out the way I meant it.''

He raised a skeptical eyebrow.

"Well, maybe it did," she admitted. "That was what I was thinking in the beginning. All we had in common when I proposed was a physical attraction. But then everything changed." She looked up at him, her eyes holding a plea for him to believe her. "At least for me it did. You weren't what I expected. The more I got to know you, the more I learned to care for you."

She cupped his face in her hands. "The day of the accident, I was trying to prove to you I could fit into your world. I know it was a childish, silly stunt. But I was trying to show off... to get your attention."

"You've had my attention for months," he admitted gruffly.

The heat in his eyes warmed her. Gently she traced the line of his scar. "I know now that the reason for my blocked memory was that I was terrified you were getting bored with our marriage and wanted out. For the past couple of months I'd sensed an uneasiness about you as if you weren't comfortable with me. I didn't want to face losing you so I tried to erase you and my feelings for you by not remembering anything."

"I was uneasy," he confessed. "You made me feel like planting roots and that was something I'd promised myself I'd never do. Besides, you are much too classy a lady for me."

She smiled. "I'm the perfect lady for you," she corrected, going up on tiptoe and kissing him lightly. "And you're the only man for me. Even when I fought remembering, I knew you were important to me. I wanted you near me."

He drew a shaky breath and wrapped his arms around her. "I was sure the reason you'd lost your memory was that you knew our marriage was a mistake and you didn't want to admit you could make such a big blunder."

The growing heat in his eyes was causing her blood to race. "The blunder I was worried about having made was falling in love with you. Stay with me, Jonah."

"Guess I'm going to have to," he said huskily. "Someone is going to have to make sure you don't go tearing around the countryside without a helmet." He drew her closer to him and kissed the tip of her nose. "Besides, I guess I . . . I've gotten used to having you around."

A wave of disappointment coursed through Eloise. She had hoped he would say he loved her. In time he will, she assured herself. He'd spent a lot of years keeping his feelings locked away. She couldn't expect him to release them all at one time. That he'd admitted to wanting to stay with her would have to be enough for now. "Could we go home?" she asked.

"Yes, home," he replied.

The warmth in his voice washed away her disappointment and filled her with hope for the future. Until now, he'd always considered the farm "her place," never "their place" and never "home." Home is where the heart is, she told herself. Then silently laughed. She was truly beginning to sound like her Aunt Sarah. Still, as she helped Jonah load her bike into his truck, she hoped that adage proved to be true.

Eloise sat in the rocking chair by the kitchen window. Six months had passed since her accident.

Aunt Sarah had left as abruptly as she'd arrived. The day after Eloise had confronted Jonah on the side of the road, Sarah had announced she felt it was time for her to go home. "You no longer need me," she said, "and I do want to check on my things. It's been a while since I've been to my own house." A glint showed in her eyes. "Then I'm going to pay your cousin Irene a visit. That girl's been on my mind for a while."

Both Eloise and Jonah had tried to convince Sarah to stay a few days longer but her aunt had been adamant. "You two need to get on with your lives. But don't you worry, I'll be back," she'd promised.

The next morning Eloise had driven Sarah to the airport. "It's just like I've always believed," her aunt had said as she prepared to board her plane. "The bigger they are, the harder they fall. And Jonah is one very big man. With the two of you to take care of each other, I'll be able to rest easy."

At the time, Eloise had been filled with hope. And during the past months, she'd felt a growing bond with Jonah. She'd thought he felt it, too. But finally, as her former life fell back into place, she had to face the truth. "I guess I was wrong," she murmured. "Obviously Jonah didn't fall as hard as Aunt Sarah thought."

Reaching down into her knitting basket, she uncovered the partially completed baby blanket that matched the already completed sweater and pair of baby booties. Before the accident she'd thought about having children.

The way Jonah had taken in Tommy and been willing to assume a fatherly role in the boy's life had convinced her he would be a good parent. But before the accident, she'd been too insecure about their marriage to broach the subject with him.

And even after the accident, her newfound openness had not given her the courage to suggest they have children. Instead she'd cautioned herself to go slowly. This morning, however, she'd finally asked him about starting a family. His response had been less than enthusiastic.

"I'm not sure I'm ready for fatherhood," he'd said. "But if you want children, it's all right with me." Then he'd said he had a lot of work to do at the gas station and left.

Her jaw firmed. The tiny sweater blurred in her vision as tears filled her eyes. "I want our children to be wanted by both of us."

Returning the sweater to the basket, she told herself to give Jonah a little more time. Meanwhile, she reminded herself, she needed to get dressed and go to her own office. She had a desk full of work waiting for her.

But the disappointment she was feeling continued to grow as she climbed the stairs. Maybe when Jonah had said he'd gotten used to having her around that was all he'd meant. He certainly hadn't made any stronger admission of his feelings for her since that day. Maybe she'd been deluding herself. Maybe she hadn't touched his heart.

She'd reached their bedroom when she heard the sound of a vehicle approaching. Looking out the window she saw his truck speeding toward the house. He was driving so fast his wheels spun gravel when he stopped.

"He must have forgotten something," she muttered, choosing to hide out in their room until he'd left again. She couldn't face him right now. Her disappointment was still too strong.

Even at this distance she saw the grim set of his jaw as he climbed out of the cab and slammed the door closed. Entering the house, he yelled, "Ellie, where are you?"

The impatience in his voice caused her stomach to knot. Dread swept through her. "I'm in the bedroom," she called back, and marveled that she sounded calm and in control. Obviously the thought of having children had caused him to have serious second thoughts about their staying married, she decided. Offspring was probably more than he wanted to commit to. "He's probably feeling closed in, suffocated, and he wants his freedom," she said under her breath, forcing herself to face facts.

Pride glistened in her eyes. This time she would let him go without a word. Clearly the lock he kept on his heart was too sturdy for her to break.

She met his gaze squarely as he came to an abrupt halt in the doorway. Indecision was etched into his features.

"Looks like the thought of children was too much for you," she said stiffly.

"It panicked me," he admitted.

She wanted to scream out of sheer disillusionment. But he'd never made her any promises he hadn't kept. "I want children," she said bluntly. "But I don't want to have them with a man who doesn't want them as much as I do." Her throat had threatened to constrict as she uttered these words. She forced herself to go on. "I guess this marriage isn't going to work out so good after all."

His gaze bored into her. "We got married for all the wrong reasons, Ellie."

Her stomach knotted tighter. Obviously he was trying to make the break easier but she wished he would just leave.

"But we stayed married for all the right ones," he finished gruffly.

She stared at him in disbelief. That wasn't what she'd expected him to say.

He moved toward her. "I love you, Ellie."

"You love me?" she choked out, half afraid she'd wanted to hear him say those words so badly she'd imagined them.

Reaching her, he tenderly stroked her cheek. "I love you and I'd love any child we might have. The truth is, I've been thinking about us having children myself but the thought of being a father is a little frightening."

"I'll hold your hand and see you through it," she promised, tears of joy flooding her eyes.

Pulling her into his arms, he held her tightly against him. "With you holding my hand, I can see my way through anything."

Happiness flooded through Eloise. She knew without any doubt that the self-protective barrier he'd kept between them was gone...every last shred of it. "I love you so much, Jonah Tavish," she said.

"We could start working on that family right now," he suggested gruffly.

"Right now sounds like a very good time," she agreed against his lips as his mouth found hers.

*   *   *   *   *

Look for the next book in Where the Heart Is *featuring Sarah Orman, coming soon from Silhouette Romance!*

Take 4 bestselling love stories FREE

Plus get a FREE surprise gift!

Special Limited-time Offer

Mail to Silhouette Reader Service™

> 3010 Walden Avenue
> P.O. Box 1867
> Buffalo, N.Y. 14269-1867

YES! Please send me 4 free Silhouette Romance™ novels and my free surprise gift. Then send me 6 brand-new novels every month, which I will receive months before they appear in bookstores. Bill me at the low price of $2.19 each plus 25¢ delivery and applicable sales tax, if any.* That's the complete price and—compared to the cover prices of $2.75 each—quite a bargain! I understand that accepting the books and gift places me under no obligation ever to buy any books. I can always return a shipment and cancel at any time. Even if I never buy another book from Silhouette, the 4 free books and the surprise gift are mine to keep forever.

215 BPA ANRP

Name	(PLEASE PRINT)	
Address	Apt. No.	
City	State	Zip

This offer is limited to one order per household and not valid to present Silhouette Romance™ subscribers. *Terms and prices are subject to change without notice. Sales tax applicable in N.Y.

USROM-94R   ©1990 Harlequin Enterprises Limited

BABY'S CHOICE

Those mischievous matchmaking babies are back, as Marie Ferrarella's Baby's Choice series continues in August with MOTHER ON THE WING (SR #1026).

Frank Harrigan could hardly explain his sudden desire to fly to Seattle. Sure, an old friend had written to him out of the blue, but there was something else.... Then he spotted Donna McCollough, or rather, she fell right into his lap. And from that moment on, they were powerless to interfere with what angelic fate had lovingly ordained.

Continue to share in the wonder of life and love, as babies-in-waiting handpick the most perfect parents, only in

Silhouette
R O M A N C E™

To order your copy of the first Baby's Choice title, *Caution: Baby Ahead* (SR #1007), please send your name, address, zip or postal code, along with a check or money order (please do not send cash) for $2.75, plus 75¢ postage and handling ($1.00 in Canada), payable to Silhouette Books, to:

In the U.S.	In Canada
Silhouette Books	Silhouette Books
3010 Walden Ave.	P. O. Box 636
P. O. Box 9077	Fort Erie, Ontario
Buffalo, NY 14269-9077	L2A 5X3

Please specify book title with your order.
Canadian residents add applicable federal and provincial taxes.

SRMF2

Beginning in August from Silhouette Romance...

by Sandra Steffen

Three sexy, single brothers bet they'll never say "I do." But the Harris boys are about to discover their vows of bachelorhood don't stand a chance against the forces of love!

Don't miss:

BACHELOR DADDY (8/94): Single father Mitch Harris gets more than just parenting lessons from his lovely neighbor, Raine McAlister.

BACHELOR AT THE WEDDING (11/94): He caught the garter, she caught the bouquet. And Kyle Harris is in for more than a brief encounter with single mom Clarissa Cohagan.

EXPECTANT BACHELOR (1/95): Taylor Harris gets the shock of his life when the stunning Gina Jenson asks him to father her child.

Find out how these confirmed bachelors finally take the marriage plunge. Don't miss WEDDING WAGER, only from

Silhouette
R O M A N C E ™

SRSS1

It's our 1000th Silhouette Romance™, and we're celebrating!

And to say "THANK YOU" to our wonderful readers, we would like to send you a

FREE AUSTRIAN CRYSTAL BRACELET

This special bracelet truly captures the spirit of CELEBRATION 1000! and is a stunning complement to any outfit! And it can be yours FREE just for enjoying SILHOUETTE ROMANCE™.

FREE GIFT OFFER

To receive your free gift, complete the certificate according to directions. Be certain to enclose the required number of proofs-of-purchase. Requests must be received no later than August 31, 1994. Please allow 6 to 8 weeks for receipt of order. Offer good while quantities of gifts last. Offer good in U.S. and Canada only.

And that's not all! Readers can also enter our...

CELEBRATION 1000! SWEEPSTAKES

In honor of our 1000th SILHOUETTE ROMANCE™, we'd like to award $1000 to a lucky reader!

As an added value every time you send in a completed offer certificate with the correct amount of proofs-of-purchase, your name will automatically be entered in our CELEBRATION 1000! Sweepstakes. The sweepstakes features a grand prize of $1000. PLUS, 1000 runner-up prizes of a FREE SILHOUETTE ROMANCE™, autographed by one of CELEBRATION 1000!'s special featured authors will be awarded. These volumes are sure to be cherished for years to come, a true commemorative keepsake.

DON'T MISS YOUR OPPORTUNITY TO WIN! ENTER NOW!

CELOFFER

CELEBRATION 1000! FREE GIFT OFFER

ORDER INFORMATION:

To receive your free AUSTRIAN CRYSTAL BRACELET, send three original proof-of-purchase coupons from any SILHOUETTE ROMANCE™ title published in April through July 1994 with the Free Gift Certificate completed, plus $1.75 for postage and handling (check or money order—please do not send cash) payable to Silhouette Books CELEBRATION 1000! Offer. Hurry! Quantities are limited.

FREE GIFT CERTIFICATE   096 KBM

Name:_____

Address:_____

City: _____ State/Prov.:_____ Zip/Postal:_____

Mail this certificate, three proofs-of-purchase and check or money order to CELEBRATION 1000! Offer, Silhouette Books, 3010 Walden Avenue, P.O. Box 9057, Buffalo, NY 14269-9057 or P.O. Box 622, Fort Erie, Ontario L2A 5X3. Please allow 4-6 weeks for delivery. Offer expires August 31, 1994.

PLUS

Every time you submit a completed certificate with the correct number of proofs-of-purchase, you are automatically entered in our CELEBRATION 1000! SWEEPSTAKES to win the GRAND PRIZE of $1000 CASH! PLUS, 1000 runner-up prizes of a FREE Silhouette Romance™, autographed by one of CELEBRATION 1000!'s special featured authors, will be awarded. No purchase or obligation necessary to enter. See below for alternate means of entry and how to obtain complete sweepstakes rules.

CELEBRATION 1000! SWEEPSTAKES
NO PURCHASE OR OBLIGATION NECESSARY TO ENTER

You may enter the sweepstakes without taking advantage of the CELEBRATION 1000! FREE GIFT OFFER by hand-printing on a 3" x 5" card (mechanical reproductions are not acceptable) your name and address and mailing it to: CELEBRATION 1000! Sweepstakes, P.O. Box 9057, Buffalo, NY 14269-9057 or P.O. Box 622, Fort Erie, Ontario L2A 5X3. Limit: one entry per envelope. Entries must be sent via First Class mail and be received no later than August 31, 1994. No liability is assumed for lost, late or misdirected mail.

Sweepstakes is open to residents of the U.S. (except Puerto Rico) and Canada, 18 years of age or older. All federal, state, provincial, municipal and local laws apply. Offer void wherever prohibited by law. Odds of winning dependent on the number of entries received. For complete rules, send a self-addressed, stamped envelope to: CELEBRATION 1000! Rules, P.O. Box 4200, Blair, NE 68009.

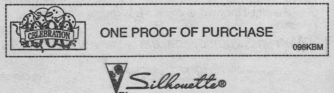

ONE PROOF OF PURCHASE

096KBM